"Stop."

At Isaiah's urgent warning, Addie froze. A midsize car slowly drove through the motel parking lot. It paused behind Isaiah's car.

"Get down."

They huddled behind the line of shrubs on the edge of the property. Addie didn't question his direction. Ollie pressed his face into her. She held him to her. Through the thinned-out branches, she saw the passenger car door open. A man stepped out, tugged at something, then threw something that was roughly the size of a softball through the window of their room. Glass shattered.

He'd thrown a grenade.

The man jumped back into the car, and the vehicle raced off, tires squealing.

The grenade detonated, obliterating room 117.

Isaiah launched himself sideways in an attempt to shield both Addie and Ollie. Debris rained down on the parking lot, showering the new snow with dust, shards of wood, plastic and glass. The room they'd rented was a gaping hole with flames consuming what was left of the interior.

If they hadn't left to eat breakfast, all three of them would be dead.

Dana R. Lynn grew up in Illinois. She met her husband at a wedding and told her parents she'd met the man she was going to marry. Nineteen months later, they were married. Today, they live in rural Pennsylvania with their three children and a variety of animals. In addition to writing, she works as a teacher for the deaf and hard of hearing, and is active in her church.

Books by Dana R. Lynn

Love Inspired Suspense

Amish Country Justice

Plain Target
Plain Retribution
Amish Christmas Abduction
Amish Country Ambush
Amish Christmas Emergency
Guarding the Amish Midwife
Hidden in Amish Country
Plain Refuge
Deadly Amish Reunion
Amish Country Threats
Covert Amish Investigation
Amish Christmas Escape
Amish Cradle Conspiracy
Her Secret Amish Past
Crime Scene Witness
Hidden Amish Target
Hunted at Christmas

Visit the Author Profile page at LoveInspired.com for more titles.

HUNTED AT CHRISTMAS

DANA R. LYNN

LOVE INSPIRED SUSPENSE
INSPIRATIONAL ROMANCE

LOVE INSPIRED® SUSPENSE
INSPIRATIONAL ROMANCE

Recycling programs
for this product may
not exist in your area.

ISBN-13: 978-1-335-59908-7

Hunted at Christmas

Copyright © 2023 by Dana Roae

For questions and comments about the quality of this book, please contact us
at CustomerService@Harlequin.com.

Love Inspired
22 Adelaide St. West, 41st Floor
Toronto, Ontario M5H 4E3, Canada
www.LoveInspired.com

Printed in U.S.A.

For the Lord your God is gracious and merciful, and will not turn away his face from you, if ye return unto him.
—*2 Chronicles* 30:9

To my family.

ONE

Thump. Bump.

Addison Bruce stilled at the sound coming from downstairs. The shirts she was placing in her son's dresser fell from her hands and landed in a pile on his bedroom floor. She didn't have any pets, and her son was still not home. Which meant only one thing. Someone was in her house. She held her breath, straining to hear above the blood pounding in her ears, listening to the quiet house with all her ability. She prayed that she was wrong and that the sound she heard was only the old creaky building protesting against the chilly December wind instead of her worst fear. What if her stalker had found her? Had he discovered that Addison Bruce and Addison Johnson were the same person?

Her eyes flew to the window. It was nearly three twenty in the afternoon. The local preschool Oliver attended had ended at two forty-five. Soon, the district school bus would rumble its way down the twisty Ohio road and stop in front of her house and let her four-year-old son off.

Another muted bump hit her ears, followed by a whispered curse, validating her fear. Her stomach wrenched itself into knots. This time, she knew exactly what had happened. Someone had stumbled and fallen over the edge of the area rug in the living room. She'd been grumbling about that rug for weeks. It was old and the one side wouldn't lay flat.

She didn't recognize the masculine voice. Whoever it was, they didn't belong in the house.

Did they know she was home? Her car was at the mechanics, getting the brakes fixed. Otherwise, it would be sitting in front of the house. Maybe someone saw an empty house on a rural road and decided to break in. That was one theory.

Or it could be him. The man who had stalked her and forced her to flee her home and hide her identity. She went by the name Addison Bruce now, using her maiden name, but it was hard to make herself respond to that name, even after six months on the run. Giving up her married name had been painful, but she needed to protect herself and Ollie. Which was why this little house on the outskirts of Sutter Springs, Ohio, had seemed so perfect. It wasn't a crowded area, but she had liked that it was close enough to Columbus that if she needed to move to the city for work or to blend in, she could.

It might have been for nothing.

No! She wouldn't think that way. She had planned for such an event.

Creeping into her own room, she grabbed the backpack she always kept ready and slid her arms into the straps, then picked up her phone, which was on silent for emergencies like this, and shoved it into the back pocket of her jeans. Her watch would buzz if a call or important text came through. Not that she had befriended many people. She'd made exactly one friend. Tricia, the woman who lived in the house closest to hers. The fewer ties she had, the better.

Sweat ran down the back of her neck, despite the coolness of the room. Maybe it wasn't someone coming after her personally, but whatever the motive, she couldn't risk waiting around.

And she definitely wasn't about to be like a

heroine in a movie and confront the person in her house. She had no way to protect herself against an invader. Besides, Ollie's safety was her first and only priority.

Lord, be my shield. Protect us.

Fortunately, she knew exactly where all the weak floorboards were placed. She'd lived in this house for the past six months and had walked across the carpeted surfaces frequently.

Slipping over to the window, she slid the glass up and used her thumbs to push the bottom latches on the screen window to release it, sliding it up as well. She paused to listen. The bottom stair groaned as if someone stepped on it.

She was almost out of time.

She reached over and grabbed the rope ladder kept behind the dresser and tossed the length of it out the window, hooking it into place on the frame. Swinging her left leg over the sill, she felt for the rungs. They swayed beneath her leg.

She didn't have time to adjust it.

The door burst open and a man wearing a ski mask charged inside, a gun in his hand. His gaze was on the bed, on the opposite side of the room, not on the side window.

That was the only thing that saved her.

She scurried out the window before he turned his head. She half climbed, half slid down the window. A screech of brakes told her the bus was stopping. Oliver was home! She jumped the last third of the ladder, her feet stumbling as they hit the ground. Snow crunched under her sneakers. Catching herself, she ran toward the front of the house.

A shout above her pushed her faster.

A gunshot echoed in the air. The blood chilled in her veins. She had to get to her child before the intruder did.

Dashing around the front of the house, she waved at the driver. He opened the door, and her son ran down the steps, his dark curls bouncing. She hurried to her grinning little boy.

"Mommy! We made Christmas cards in school today!"

"Sweetie, hold my hand, we need to hurry." She gripped his small mittened hand in hers. She didn't even have a coat on. At least he was bundled up. And she did have on shoes with good tread. "Someone is in the house. We need to run."

Ollie's bottom lip thrust out and quivered, but he didn't argue. They'd gone through this drill many times since they'd moved in. He had his backpack on, which meant he had a change of clothes and his stuffed doggie, Bowie, that he carried everywhere.

They had to find a way to get to the police. She winced. Her husband had been a police officer in Pennsylvania. He'd been shot and killed in the line of duty when Oliver had been four months old. Three years later, what remained of her life had been turned upside down when someone began stalking her. She never found out who.

She led Ollie off the side of the road and onto the path that went behind the houses. She had marked out a little trail that led to her neighbor Tricia's house over the past six months. Although most of the path couldn't be seen from the road, Tricia had become used to seeing her neighbors and never questioned why they weren't going to the front door.

This was part of Addie's plan. She needed a place to stop and plan if the worst happened.

Like today.

Jogging up to Tricia's back door, she rang the doorbell. The chimes echoed through the house.

Then she waited, tapping her foot rapidly on the cement. Tricia's car had been in the driveway when she'd jogged past earlier in the afternoon. That didn't mean much, though.

Sometimes her neighbor got a ride to work with her boyfriend, who worked at the same place. Her gaze swept the horizon. She wasn't naïve enough to think she'd lost the man coming after them. Best-case scenario, he had taken off in the opposite direction after them. Even if that were what happened, it wouldn't be long before he realized he'd gone the wrong way and turn around to follow them.

Or he could be breathing down their necks while they stood there, waiting.

Of course, if it was just a robbery, he might not give chase. After all, he was wearing a ski mask. It wasn't like she'd seen his face and could identify him.

But he had charged into the room like he was looking for her. Her stomach cramped, nearly bowing her over. She'd come so far, uprooted their lives; would it all end here? Had the man she'd run to escape finally found her?

A motor was coming up the road.

She had to get Ollie hidden. Reaching into her pocket, she drew out the key Tricia had given her after she'd locked herself out of her house two months ago.

"If you ever need to, you can stay in my house until you can get back into yours. Don't worry if I'm home or not. I trust you."

The irony was Tricia trusted Addison Bruce, not Addison Johnson. She had no clue who she was really helping.

Slipping the key into the lock, Addie led Ollie into the garage and closed the door behind her. "We need to hide here, honey, until it's safe."

Ollie's big brown eyes flooded with tears. He burrowed into her side, his small frame shaking. She hugged him close and waited. Too late, it occurred to her what she'd done. She'd sought refuge in her friend's home, potentially bringing danger to Tricia's doorstep.

And if her pursuer figured out where she'd gone, she and her son would be effectively trapped.

Isaiah Bender caught a glimpse of a dark-haired woman leading a small boy bundled up in winter gear before they disappeared behind a house. Both had on backpacks. The way the woman kept glancing over her shoulder helped him fill in the blanks. She was scared.

He parked his car along the shoulder of the dirt road, careful not to pull too close to the edge. The recent snowfall blurred the line between the shoulder and the ditch on the other side.

Getting out of the car, he glanced again at

his phone, narrowing his gaze on the images he'd been sent.

Addison Johnson. Her dark hair floated loose and straight to her shoulders. The pictures showed her profile, although she had been slightly turned away from the camera as she used a pilfered bank card and stole money from an outdoor ATM. He'd seen the edge of her eyes in one shot. The irises were dark, and the lashes were long and sooty. She had a slightly upturned nose.

Yes, he'd know that woman if he saw her in person, regardless of if he had a full view of her face. She needed to be brought to justice. Addison had been charged with multiple counts of larceny and fraud before she'd vanished. Isaiah was the bounty hunter hired to bring her in. Once he handed her over to the law, he'd be paid his bounty. The bail bondsman who'd contracted him two months ago to find her and bring her in had posted a hefty one hundred thousand dollars bail to ensure her appearance in court. He had hired Isaiah to locate her, promising him ten percent of the bail posted. Since Isaiah had no other cases at the moment, he'd been able to devote all his attention to locating this fugitive.

Ten thousand dollars was a good sum of

money, but Isaiah never kept it all. He would keep what he needed to live. The rest he'd donate to charities, specifically those that funded efforts for the recovery of runaway and missing children and that helped victims of PTSD and domestic violence.

This case was the only reason he'd returned to Sutter Springs, Ohio. He hadn't been back in the area for fourteen years. Not since he'd packed a few meager belongings and left his Amish home, the week after he turned seventeen.

He didn't plan on sticking around, either. He'd do his job and leave. A pang struck him for a moment. His older brother Micah had left the Amish community a couple of years before Isaiah had. He hadn't seen him since. When Isaiah had left, he'd broken contact with his parents and his other two brothers, Zeke and Gideon. His sister, Christina, had vanished long ago. Her abduction was the beginning of his life spiraling out of sync with his Amish family.

He missed them. Every day. But sometimes, you really couldn't go back. Between what had happened to Christina, and the preventable death of his best friend, Raymond, an anger had burned inside him. It had gradually changed into a determination to bring to justice those who broke the law and caused others harm for monetary gain.

Such as Addison Johnson.

He glanced at where she'd disappeared and frowned.

The information he'd been given had never mentioned a child. His determination to bring her in doubled. Obviously, the minor was in danger. He'd have to ensure the little boy was taken care of and safe before he put this case behind him.

Isaiah avoided children as much as possible. Not because he didn't like them. No, actually it was the opposite. He had a soft spot for them, and an old wound that had never healed. A wound that was twenty-seven years old.

He winced, trying to rip his mind away from the day his family had first splintered. The day his two-year-old sister Christina had disappeared without a trace. It was the first of several tragedies that had ruined the tranquility of his Amish home and made it impossible for him to remain there.

Movement distracted him from his reverie. Something was happening inside the house.

Getting out of his car, he paused and waited for an SUV to drive past. The driver was going slow, probably because of the slippery roads. And the lack of snow tires. The second the SUV moved past him, Isaiah shot across the street. He veered away from the front door and circled around the back, where he'd seen Addison disappear. A flurry of footprints marred the pristine snow.

Three sets of prints. A small set of children's boots that must have belonged to the little boy. A set of size six or seven prints that were probably sneakers—and would be his fugitive. And a large set of heavy boots. Those ones appeared freshest.

Someone entered the home after Addison. Had she been colluding with others? Had Isaiah stumbled upon her accomplice, too?

Someone with as many criminal charges against her as Addison did usually work with someone else, at least in his experience. He'd need to proceed with care. Patting his side, he felt the slight bulge of his gun. Normally, he'd approach with his weapon at the ready. Now, he hesitated. There was a child in the building. He couldn't risk going in armed when an innocent was involved.

Removing his hand from his gun, he edged toward the door. He'd listen at the door for a moment and maybe try to sneak in and surprise her rather than get himself killed in an ambush. He'd made that mistake once before during his first year as a bounty hunter, earning himself a two-inch-long scar down the left side of his face from his ear to his jaw. He hadn't made that mistake since.

A sudden crash followed by a woman's terrified shriek and a child crying changed his plans. Isaiah tried the door, jiggling the doorknob twice. It was locked. He rammed his right shoulder into the door, putting his entire body into it. The door shuddered and opened, the doorknob falling to the garage floor with a clang.

Charging into the garage, he interrupted a man with a ski mask struggling with his fugitive, a gun lying behind him on the floor. Evidently, she'd disarmed him.

Isaiah didn't know if this was an attack, or a partnership gone bad. All he knew was a woman—whether she was innocent or guilty didn't matter—and a young child were in danger.

He stepped forward and ripped the man away from her. The masked man had bulk in his favor. He stood at least four inches over Isaiah's own five foot ten inches and outweighed him by a good twenty pounds. The man launched himself at Isaiah. The force of his attack would have decimated an unskilled opponent.

Isaiah, however, had mixed martial arts training, thanks to a stint in the Marines, and was stubborn to his soul. He wasn't about to let a minor thing like his opponent's weight discourage him. When the man went for him, he came up under his arms and twisted one behind his back. As the man went down, he used the steel toe of his boot to put pressure against the sensitive spot at the back of his knee. Within a minute, he had the other man down on the floor, sitting next to the wall with his hands cuffed behind his back. He yanked the ski mask off his head. He tightened his jaw to keep his face from betraying the shock slamming through his mind.

Darryl Hughes, a man wanted for several murders spanning across the southern half of Ohio, glared back at him, a cruel smirk twisting his mouth. He was also known for his strength and endurance. Isaiah couldn't believe he'd subdued the felon.

Who had Addison Johnson gotten herself involved with?

He turned to look at his fugitive. She huddled next to the child, her arms encasing him in a protective embrace, crooning and comforting him as only a mother could. She raised her eyes to his. Instead of the dark irises he'd expected, twin glacial green orbs seared into him, bravely holding his gaze despite the fear simmering in their depths.

He hadn't expected to feel sympathy or pity for a fugitive. Or a spark of admiration at her grit. He shoved it away. There was nothing admirable about a criminal, one who took advantage of the weak and gullible.

The man on the floor growled and hurled vicious abuse at him. He kept his face blank, although inside, he secretly wished for a gag or a muzzle. No child should have to hear the ugly words pouring from his mouth.

He turned away and found Addison had cuddled her son closer, her hands covering his ears.

If Isaiah had thought the child might have been stolen, one look at their two faces canceled that idea. The little guy had the same green eyes as his mother, as well as the same mouth and nose. But his dark hair curled, unlike Addison's.

"Are you Addison Johnson?"

Her eyes widened and dismay fluttered across her face, then it was gone. He could have missed it if he hadn't been looking right at her.

"Are you a police officer?" Addison asked. Her soft contralto voice surprised him. It was gentle and held a whisper of the South. She didn't answer his question.

Although he understood her reservation, the air of hope in her question puzzled him. Why would she want him to be a cop? Surely, a woman with her rap sheet would want anyone except a cop to find her. He had to be reading her wrong.

"Bounty hunter." He slammed his lips shut, regretting his lack of control. He was the one who should be asking the questions. He had always been skilled at maintaining his control, regardless of the circumstances. Something about the pretty brunette threw him off kilter. In his mind, he saw the video he'd been sent. He couldn't put his finger on it, but something felt off.

Isaiah had learned to trust his instincts. He didn't know what it was that bothered him. Yet. He'd figure it out. Then he'd take her to the police station and let them take care of her. Once they handed him a receipt to verify he'd handed her over, he could return to collect from the person who had hired him to capture her.

Except…

What would happen to the kid? His heart twisted like someone had pulled it from his chest and wrung it. He didn't want to be responsible for the suffering of a child. Not to mention things weren't feeling right. Isaiah had been living by his wits long enough to have learned to trust his gut. Right now, his gut told him something was off. Before he made any decisions, he needed to figure out what it was.

People died when they acted prematurely.

He'd seen it happen before. It wouldn't happen again; not if he could stop it.

TWO

Isaiah forced his doubts from his mind and focused on doing what he knew needed to be done. Once he'd dealt with the immediate danger, he could take the time to sift through the information he had and decipher fact from fiction.

"I have to call the police and report this guy," Isaiah said, watching her expression, waiting for the flash of unease. It never came. Something about the steadiness in her gaze made him squirm internally. He dropped his gaze to the child in her arms.

Addison held her little boy tight for a second before rising to her feet and placing herself squarely between the child and both men, although she kept a solid grip on her son's small hand. Her attention shifted from Isaiah to Darryl Hughes, who still resembled a grizzly bear, even seated on the ground and contained with his hands behind his back. Her stance stiffened. Wariness crept into her expression. She shivered.

Interesting. She didn't fear Isaiah even though he represented the law, but the apprehension in her gaze as she looked at Darryl was unmistakable. What kind of criminal didn't fear capture by the law? This case was growing weirder by the moment.

He needed to find out what exactly was going on.

"Ma'am, how do you know this man?"

Her head jerked in his direction and her jaw dropped. She braced her shoulders, fury blazing in her eyes. Her pale cheeks flooded with hot color. She was ready for a fight. "Know him? How can you ask that? The man was trying to kill me when you broke through the door. I've never seen him before. All I know is he broke into my house and tried to shoot me. I climbed out through a window, grabbed my son and came here to hide. He found me." She tossed a fear-tinted glare at Darryl.

Isaiah narrowed his eyes, not sure he bought the story. "And you've never seen him before?"

She huffed an aggravated sigh. "Pretty sure."

"Pretty sure? Meaning it's possible you have

seen him? Which is it?" Even to his own ears, his voice sounded harsh.

She hesitated. He could see her weighing in her head whether she should say something or keep quiet. She sent a quick glance to her son. That seemed to decide it for her. "I lived in Pennsylvania before this. Someone was stalking me. When I got scared that my son would be hurt, I took off. That was several years ago. I never got a good look at the stalker. It might have been him."

The man on the floor fought against his restraints. Leaning to the left, he spat on the ground, the ultimate show of defiance and contempt. "I didn't stalk you in Pennsylvania."

Isaiah could believe that. Darryl Hughes was a hired killer. If he stalked someone, it would only be until he had the go-ahead to make the kill shot. Isaiah tensed to keep the shudder in his soul at the mindless, cold violence at bay.

Turning his mind back to what she'd said, he frowned. Isaiah had never heard about a stalking incident involving her, and he decided he didn't care. He turned back to Addison. "Why did you run here, to this house, today?"

She'd been able to get into the house with no problem. She obviously had a plan. And where was the owner?

She ran a shaking hand through her straight hair. "My friend Tricia lives here. She gave me a key so I could come here if I locked myself out of my house again, or if I needed something. Sometimes I feed her cat while she's on a trip. She can tell you herself when she gets home from work."

How many times had she locked herself out of her house? He let the fleeting question go. It was irrelevant.

"Her car is in the driveway. Are you sure she's not inside?"

She was already shaking her head. "She gets a ride to work with her boyfriend."

The man on the floor laughed, a harsh grating sound. When she looked at him, he sneered at her. "I'm not the only person who'll be coming for you. Someone wants you out of their way. That's why I'm here. There's a fifty thousand reward for your death. I intend to collect it." His biceps bulged and he grunted. Isaiah heard something crack a second before Darryl's arms flew out from behind him, broken cuffs dangling from his right wrist. In a flash, he fell on his gun and rolled on his back, aiming it at her.

She screamed and pushed the child behind her, a mother's instinctive attempt to defend her child.

Isaiah ripped his gun from his holster and fired, the bullet catching the hired killer in the wrist. The gun dropped to the ground. Isaiah wrestled with the larger man. They both fell to the ground, bouncing off the ping-pong table in the middle of the room. When Darryl stilled, he backed away. He'd been knocked unconscious. He'd probably hit his head on the ping-pong table. Isaiah had never seen a garage set up like a game room before.

Time to deal with his fugitive.

He pivoted to face her and met her slightly dazed eyes. Her glance fell to the man on the floor before she jerked it back to Isaiah's face.

"Mommy." The little boy tugged at her shirt, claiming her focus. "Can we go home now? I'm hungry."

She sagged, relieved.

"Okay, sweetie." She turned to Isaiah. "I live next door if the police have any questions." She started to move toward the door.

"Hold it."

She turned and raised an eyebrow. "What? I need to feed my son. He hasn't eaten since lunch time."

Isaiah lifted his phone to his ear and called the police, letting them know he had a man wanted for murder in custody. When he hung up, he faced her again. He'd chased her down and wasn't leaving her now that he'd found her.

He approached her and spoke in a low voice.

"I didn't come for him." He indicated the man on the floor. "I came after you. Addison Johnson, you're wanted for larceny and fraud. I've been hired to track you down and ensure you appear in court."

Her eyes widened. All the color drained from her face. He'd never met anyone who could act that shocked so well. For a moment, doubt twisted in his gut. But only a moment. He steeled himself against it. He'd seen some of the worst criminals. People who could lie their way out of any mess.

She was no different.

"I didn't do anything wrong." Her voice was low. "I left my home in Pennsylvania to escape a stalker. My husband was a police officer killed in the line of duty. I legally changed my name back to my maiden name so it would be harder for the stalker to find me." Her chin rose and she faced him, her gaze looking directly into his. "Addison Johnson hasn't existed for over six months."

Addison whirled away and gathered her hungry child close. The words from the two men pounded in her head. She was wanted by a bounty hunter. And a killer. There had to be a way she could prove her innocence. What if they took her child from her?

When the bounty hunter and the thug on the floor were fighting, she had wanted to run. But where would she go? With Ollie, there was no where she could get fast enough. Nowhere to hide.

And it would only make her look guilty. Plus, there was a chance whoever chased her would shoot her. No, she couldn't take that chance.

Her phone beeped. She froze, her blood icing over. She knew that sound. Although her phone was on silent, her son's continuous glucose monitor was warning her that his glucose levels were outside the normal range. The app required that the device it was connected to allowed it to give alerts through the Do Not Disturb settings. She had it connected to the cloud so she would get readings even while he was at school. When it went off, she knew Ollie needed something to eat, but more importantly, he needed an insulin injection.

Footsteps approached her. Her grip on her son tightened. She glanced up into the cold eyes of the bounty hunter. Was he a killer?

He didn't look like one. Even when he'd taken down the other man, he hadn't used his obvious strength and skill to injure the man, only subdue him.

Voices were right outside the door.

"That's the police," the bounty hunter murmured. "Go stand over there in that corner." He pointed to the far side of the garage. "Don't say anything. And don't try to leave."

"I have to check my son." She kept the panic out of her voice with supreme effort. Her phone continued to give a single beep every three seconds. "He's a type 1 diabetic. That beeping is his continuous glucose monitor. I have his insulin kit. And Ollie needs to eat something. I have something quick in my bag. It's over there. He'll need something more soon, but it should be enough to hold him over until then."

She pointed to the backpack she'd dropped.

His expression remained stoic, but she noticed a subtle softening around his eyes. He walked over and grabbed the bag. While she watched, shocked, he opened it and peered inside before holding it out to her. "Don't try anything."

She took the bag from him, fuming. Don't try anything? What did he think she'd do? He was the one with the gun. Maybe he thought she had some kind of weapon hidden in her bag. She pulled out her emergency kit. The insulin was kept on ice. She had enough for two days, but she'd have to grab more. If only she'd been able to get the rest from the refrigerator before they ran!

Quickly, she prepped the area and gave her small child the injection. The needle was so tiny, and he was so used to the process, he didn't flinch at all. All at once, she was overwhelmed with her love for Ollie. She kissed the top of his head and grabbed the string cheese she had packed and handed it to him. He scarfed it down. She knew it wasn't enough, but it would keep him going for a bit longer.

Isaiah shifted his stance. She looked into his inscrutable face. She might have thought him heartless, except for the way his haunted eyes tightened.

He met her glance squarely, though. "Look, I'll do what I can to hurry this process so he can eat something else soon. I promise. For now, please just do what I tell you."

She found herself following his instructions, her mind a whirl of confusion. Was he planning on handing her over? Her intuition told her no. She knew nothing about bounty hunters. Maybe he had to deliver her to someone specific.

Since he was letting the police into the garage, and they were effectively blocking her escape, she'd bide her time. For Ollie. But if she could, she'd try to escape.

She'd no sooner thought that than the man caught her glance. "Don't think about trying to escape," he said.

Of course, he'd be expecting for her to make an attempt to run. For the moment, there was nothing she could do. She led Ollie over to a couch against the far side of the garage. Unlike most garages, Tricia's wasn't used to store vehicles or tools. She used it for parties and games. The garage had chairs, a couch and the ping-pong table the two men had fallen against earlier. Although her bubbly neighbor had invited her to several events, including a large Labor Day party and a Fall Fest party, she'd declined. The fewer people she interacted with, the safer she'd be. That had been her strategy.

Of course, she hadn't counted on someone having a contract out on her. She shook her head, shock reverberating through her mind. She'd never even had a speeding ticket. How had she gained this kind of infamy?

The obvious answer was someone had stolen her identity.

She was vaguely aware of the conversation

between the bounty hunter and the two police officers. He identified himself as Isaiah Bender.

A scuffle across the room caught her attention. The man who'd tried to kill her was conscious again. The cops, one an officer and the other a lieutenant according to their rank insignias, were pulling Darryl Hughes to his feet. The female lieutenant read him his rights.

He didn't go willingly. She covered Ollie's ears again, trying to protect him from hearing the man's foul language.

"Who is that?"

The officer pointed in her direction. She'd ducked her head, tugging her son closer. The poor kid. She could hear his stomach growling, but he wasn't complaining. This afternoon had terrified him. Hopefully, he hadn't been too traumatized by the events of the past hour.

Isaiah dipped his chin in her direction. "She's the neighbor. She came over to see the owner of the house, who is apparently not here. Mr. Hughes attacked her."

Addie clenched her jaw to keep it from falling open. Isaiah hadn't lied, but he had deliberately left out important information. She couldn't figure out what his game was. Why he hadn't told them he thought she was some kind of hardened criminal. A fugitive he was going to drag back to face her day in court. She nearly snorted.

"I'd like to let her go home soon. Her little boy is hungry," Isaiah commented. "He's diabetic."

She held her breath. She clutched her son's hand in her own.

All eyes settled on Ollie.

"We'll book Mr. Hughes then come over and interview her," the lieutenant decided. "That way she can feed her child. We don't want him to be scared."

"I'll walk them over," Isaiah said.

"Mommy," Ollie whispered, shoving his face into her side. "I need to go potty."

She bit her lip. "Can you wait five minutes?"

He shook his head, his face rubbing against her. She glanced up at the circle of law enforcement surrounding her. "Can we go inside the house? Tricia won't mind. She gave me a key so we could come in at any time if she wasn't here."

She could see they wanted to say no, but Ollie's woeful eyes made them hesitate and give in. She'd been the victim of those big green eyes enough times to know how hard it was to say no to him.

"Sure."

She moved to the inside of the house, aware of Isaiah the bounty hunter treading on her heels. She wasn't going to ditch him anytime soon. Sighing, she shoved open the door between the garage and the house.

She slipped her shoes off on the mat inside the door and waited for Ollie to kick off his little boots. Isaiah entered and began to march across the floor. She pressed her lips together, biting back the urge to reprimand him.

A second later, guilt surged inside. He was looking around corners. She recognized the move. Her husband had done that every time they came home, checking to make sure the house was safe before letting his wife enter.

Isaiah opened the bathroom door and checked it out, then nodded. Ollie ran inside and closed the door behind him. An awkward silence fell between them as they waited.

Suddenly, she straightened. "Do you hear that?"

Why was she talking to him? He was the enemy.

"Hear what?" He frowned, looking at her suspiciously.

Before she could respond, she heard it again. A low, angry meow. "That's Tricia's cat. He's in the basement."

Puzzled, she walked to the basement door. "Tricia never lets him down there. I'll bet he snuck through when she opened it. She'll be upset if she finds out he got stuck there."

She opened the door, and the cat dashed into the kitchen, his fur sticking straight up and his tail puffed twice its normal size with anger. Or fear.

"What's wrong, Khan?" She reached out her hand to pet the large gray tiger-striped cat. He hissed and backed away, a low growl coming from deep in his throat. "This is not normal behavior. Khan is the friendliest cat I've ever seen."

Isaiah moved to her side.

She chose to ignore him. Moving to close the door, she frowned. "Something's at the bottom of the stairs."

He reached out and flipped on the light.

Addie took one look at the body at the bottom of the stairs in a pool of blood, and everything went black.

THREE

Addison pitched forward. Sheer reflex had Isaiah leaping forward and catching the woman before she crashed headfirst down the steep stairs. The unexpected dead weight sent him stumbling back two steps. His left heel slipped over the edge of the top of the staircase. Wrapping his arms tightly around her, he steadied them both. Her soft brown hair tickled his nose. It smelled like coconut. Blowing the hair away from his nose, he shifted her so he had a better grip. It wouldn't do any good if both of them tumbled down the stairs and got injured.

At this point, he wasn't even concerned about messing up the evidence trail. His goal for the moment was getting her away from the current danger and making sure her son had what he needed. No matter how jaded he'd become over the years, children remained his weak spot. He would do anything to protect a child.

Pulling her away from the basement entrance, he kicked the door closed with his foot and called out to the cops in the garage. He wanted to carry Addison to the couch he'd seen around the corner, but the whole house now had potentially become a secondary crime scene. He'd only seen the woman's body from the waist down. That wasn't enough to tell if she was dead or seriously injured. Guessing from the amount of blood he'd seen, he was pretty sure she was dead.

One thing was certain. Addison hadn't had time to murder the woman without her son being aware before Darryl had entered the house after her.

Tricia had never gone to work that day. Nor would she ever go to work again. He recalled the way Darryl Hughes had laughed when Addison had mentioned her friend was at work. How long had she been lying there? There hadn't been a noticeable smell, so probably not more than a day. Addison had also mentioned a boyfriend.

Before he could continue with that train of thought, Lieutenant Kathy Bartlett and Officer Alan Yates hurried into the kitchen. Officer Yates's glance landed on the unconscious woman in Isaiah's arms before flying to his face, eyes wide.

"What's the problem?" the lieutenant demanded, her eyes scanning the area, searching for danger.

Isaiah jerked his head in the direction of the basement. "The cat was stuck in the basement. I looked down the stairs and saw a body. I'm nearly certain she's dead. Addison saw the body and passed out without identifying the woman, but I'm guessing it's Tricia, the owner of the house."

The lieutenant slipped through the basement door. She returned a minute later. "She's dead, all right."

Officer Yates swallowed audibly, his Adam's apple bobbing in his throat. The color seeped from his face.

Great. A rookie. This was probably his first homicide. Lieutenant Bartlett's head jerked around to watch her colleague. "You okay, Alan? I can deal with this."

He shook his head and visibly braced himself. "I can handle it. Don't worry about me."

Isaiah's respect for the rookie grew. Dealing with murder wasn't easy. Death of any sort could mess with your mind.

"I'm going to take her into the kitchen. I'll watch for the boy, too."

The lieutenant nodded. "Don't touch anything you don't have to."

Duh. He held the snarky comment inside. He swung Addison into his arms and moved into the kitchen and carefully lowered her onto the linoleum flooring, taking care to set her behind the island so Ollie wouldn't be alarmed when he returned. It was cool to the touch. He frowned. Maybe he should have put his coat down first. What was he thinking? She was a fugitive, and he was treating her like she was fine china.

Except he wasn't completely convinced she was the fugitive in question. Despite her outward similarity to the woman caught on video. Isaiah had been in this line of work for a long time. He had seen a lot of cases that weren't as cut and dried as they should have been.

Bottom line, he'd never forgive himself if he handed over an innocent woman, left a young child with a debilitating disease in the care of strangers and collected his money and left. In his mind, even though he had a legal contract, that would be abandonment.

He couldn't do it.

Down the hall, he heard the toilet flush behind the closed bathroom door, followed by the rush of running water. He checked to make sure Addison was still out cold. She was. The large gray cat with black tiger stripes padded over as if he were a king and majestically curled himself against her side. Isaiah stepped around the island and waited for the little boy.

Ollie skipped out of the bathroom and ran toward him, slowing when his mom didn't appear. Panic twisted his face. "Mommy! Mommy!"

Isaiah dropped to one knee, holding his hands out to calm the youngster. "Hey, buddy, it's okay. Your mom is fine."

"Where is she?" Ollie's bottom lip pushed out and quivered.

"She fainted. I'm waiting for her to wake up. Come on, you can wait with me."

Some of the panic left the child's face. He placed his hand in Isaiah's. "I fainted before. If my blood sugar gets too low, I gotta drink orange juice so I don't faint. Does Mommy need orange juice?"

Something inside him melted. If he was not careful, this kid would worm his way right into his heart.

"Maybe she'll drink some when you guys get back to your house. Okay?"

When they rounded the corner of the island, Ollie ripped his hand from Isaiah's and ran the last three steps to his mother's side. He dropped down beside her, his little face pale. His small hands reached out and dragged the large cat into his arms. Then he snuggled into her side where the feline had been. "Wake up, Mommy."

A sudden lump formed in Isaiah's throat. He swallowed three times before it dissolved.

"Mr. Bender."

He turned to Lieutenant Bartlett. "Isaiah."

She nodded. "Isaiah. We're going to need to bring the crime scene unit in, and when they're done, the crime scene cleaners will be allowed in. It's going to be an hour or two yet."

"She was murdered then."

"She was. I think her murderer has been hiding here for at least a day. Maybe more."

Until that moment, he had harbored the slight hope that she had fallen down the stairs. It hadn't been likely, but for someone to deliberately take another life for a reason other than self-defense or defense of another, he still couldn't wrap his mind around it, despite his time in the military and the years he'd been working alongside the law. He figured it was his Amish upbringing that kept him from becoming completely desensitized to the brutality of the world he lived in.

Despite everything he had seen in his life, some things still shocked him.

Addie lurched to a sitting position, a cry of horror escaping her. A warm body snuggled against her. Oliver. Khan was purring like a freight train in his embrace. They were in the middle of the kitchen. She scooped him up, cat and all, in her arms.

Isaiah stood near the doorway, blocking the entrance to the basement.

"Tricia." Her throat closed, squeezing off the words. She swallowed, blinking the tears from her eyes. "Is she…"

She couldn't bring herself to say the word *dead*.

Isaiah seemed to understand. He moved closer to her, stopping a foot away. He shoved his hands into his pockets. "She is. I'm sorry. They—the police—are down there now. The coroner and the crime scene investigation team have been called. It will take a while to process the scene. I have permission to bring you back to your house once you're able to go. The police will have questions once they're done here."

"That man?"

"He's on his way to the police station. He won't bother you again."

There'd be others. The man who had tried to kill her had said there was a price on her head. She couldn't imagine why. This whole situation confused her. She needed to get home and pack. Obviously, she couldn't remain where she was anymore.

But first, she needed to go home.

She released her son and pushed herself to her feet. Then she hesitated. "What about the cat?"

She couldn't take Khan and run again. But she hated to abandon him.

"I don't know. He'll be cared for until the family decide what to do."

"If they don't want him…" She was going to say she'd take the cat, but she had no clue what she'd be doing. Did Isaiah Bender still believe she was a criminal? He was being gentle with her if he did. A sudden thought occurred to her.

"I had nothing to do with—" Again, she couldn't complete her sentence. And not only because of her grief and shock. She didn't want Oliver to catch the drift of what was happening.

He nodded. "I figured. You were genuinely

shocked to see Tricia. If I hadn't caught you, you would have ended up at the bottom of the stairs. There's no way you could have known I'd react quick enough to catch you."

At least he believed her innocent of that.

He glanced at the little boy shoving his tiny feet into the winter boots at the door. "We'll talk when we get to your house."

Addison had never considered herself particularly passive. She tended to argue and push back when she felt things weren't fair. In this instance, though, she went along with his suggestion to keep her son as far out of this sordid business as possible.

Zipping Ollie's coat, she pushed her feet into her sneakers and gathered up their backpacks. Within a minute, the trio left the house and were on their way back to her home.

The wind had picked up, and the temperature had dropped while they were away from the house. She shivered violently. Her toes grew more numb with each step she took. By the time they were halfway between her house and Tricia's, her teeth were chattering so hard, she was sure the noise was echoing in the still air.

She jumped, shocked, when Isaiah's coat dropped over her shoulders. She had been so focused on moving her feet, she hadn't noticed him removing it. It was still warm from his body heat. If it hadn't been so cold, she might have rejected it with a snippy comment. After all, he planned on hauling her in front of some court.

She was too cold to argue.

She was still intent on escaping him if she couldn't convince him of her innocence. Now wasn't the time. He was stronger, and with Ollie, she knew she'd be slower. She had to be smart about how she handled this situation.

Nothing would change until she managed to get back to the house. With a renewed sense of purpose, she plunged ahead, leaning into the wind.

"Mommy, my feet are cold."

She sighed, her breath puffing in front of her face. Whatever hold Ollie had on his tongue had loosened since they'd left Tricia's house. Every twenty steps or so, he'd uttered a complaint. He was cold or hungry or tired, or he wanted to see Khan again. She couldn't blame the child. He'd been so good, and today had been an exhausting one.

Finally, they arrived home. She unlocked the front door. Isaiah made them wait while he searched the house. This time, she held her son back and let him do it, her shoulders tight when he left her sight.

She could run now, she thought, while they waited. Except her son was exhausted. And it was dark. And she had no vehicle. Before she could think further, Isaiah popped back into view and gestured for them to enter.

Oliver flew inside the house and headed for the kitchen.

"Grab a banana!" she called after him. "I'll fix dinner in a few."

Normally, Thursdays were their day to indulge in a special pizza she'd discovered with a crust that was made from cauliflower instead of white flour, sugar-free frozen yogurt and maybe a special movie, since he didn't have preschool on Fridays. Tonight was going to break that pattern. It couldn't be helped. Nothing could have prepared her for today's attack.

Or Tricia's murder.

She tore her thoughts from the memory of her friend lying motionless on the cold basement floor, squeezing her lids shut to force the image aside. She'd see it in her dreams for the rest of her life.

"Hey." A low voice called to her. She opened her eyes and turned to see Isaiah looming at her side. He stood in the shadows. It was too dark to see his eyes, or to read his expression. But his voice… Was that compassion? "The police will do what they can to make sure justice is found."

"Was it him?"

"Darryl Hughes? The man who attacked you?"

"Yeah."

He shrugged. "It would make sense. I think he'd been using her house as a base while he spied on you. The police seemed to think she was killed yesterday."

She shook her head slowly. "This is like a bad movie. I have a hit out on me. And a bounty hunter is after me. There has to be a way I can prove that I am not the person you're after."

He hesitated. "I don't know about that. But something you said interested me. You said you've been using your maiden name for six months now."

She nodded. "I had my name and Oliver's last name changed to Bruce because I thought I had attracted a stalker. It never occurred to me there was a hit out on me. When someone broke into my home while I was at work one day, it was the last straw. My neighbor got suspicious and called the police. The stalker was gone when they got there, but they found where he'd hidden. He had been in Ollie's room. Two weeks later, the police hadn't found the man, so I left town."

And she had never gone back to Pennsylvania or contacted anyone from her former life. Not even her mother-in-law.

"Why don't you go and fix your son dinner? I need to check on something."

She huffed. Typical man. Giving her orders in her own house.

She wandered into the kitchen and reached into the refrigerator, pulling out the eggs and cheddar cheese. She cracked open four eggs. Her hand hesitated, and then she added two more. Within minutes, she had several fluffy omelets cooking, filled with spinach and green peppers. In another pan, she fried up some turkey bacon. Oliver needed protein.

"Mommy, are we having breakfast?"

She leaned over and kissed his head. "We are. Isn't that fun?"

"Yes. Pizza would be funner."

"I know. But we can't do pizza tonight. Soon, Ollie. Soon."

Hopefully, that was a promise she'd be able to keep.

FOUR

The answering machine light blinked at her as she turned away. She had one new message. Pressing Play, she returned the eggs to the refrigerator.

"Hi, Addie. It's Kevin from Drummond Auto. Your car is ready. I'll leave the keys under the floor mat." He rattled off a sum. "You can leave a check in the drop box."

Good. She didn't like being without a vehicle. The first time Kevin had told her she could pick up her car after hours and leave a check, she'd been floored. That was a lot of trust to have in a stranger. But that was the way people operated in Sutter Springs. She'd dropped her car off for an oil change and had him replace her tires before, so the arrangement didn't strike her as that unusual anymore.

The bacon was ready. She placed it on a plate covered with a paper towel, carried it to the table, and straightened the tablecloth while she was there. All of her furniture was secondhand. She hadn't known how long they'd be able to stay, so there was no point in blowing money on possessions they might one day have to leave behind.

That possibility had never seemed as real as it did today.

"Oliver," Addie called her son and set the plates on the table.

His feet pounded down the hall to the kitchen. No matter how often she reprimanded him about running in the house, he couldn't seem to keep his feet from moving at full speed. She grinned as the steps stopped suddenly three seconds before he entered the room at a sedate walk.

"You know," she teased, "you're supposed to walk the whole way, not only when I can see you."

His eyes widened. "How did you know I runned?"

"Because I'm your mommy, and mommies know a lot of stuff." She leaned down and brushed his hair from his forehead with an affectionate gesture. "Wash up for dinner."

"Okay. I can tell the man it's dinner time."

"No!" she snapped out before she could stop herself. When he looked at her, mouth open in a wide O, she sighed. She didn't want to frighten the child, but she still didn't know this bounty hunter enough to trust him. Especially considering the fact that he might cause them more harm than the stalker had.

Running wasn't an option at the moment. The police were next door. Plus, Isaiah would hear her if she and Ollie planned to leave. He had set some kind of alarm on the door when they'd come in. So if they made a move to leave, he'd know. He said it was for their protection, but she had her doubts.

And then there was Ollie. Since they'd returned home, the temperature had dropped to twenty degrees outside. It was too cold to take a small boy out without having a vehicle. His boots were soaked. She had them on the heated boot dryer, and his wet coat, hat and gloves were in the dryer.

And then there was the problem of his insulin. While leaving earlier had no doubt saved their lives, she didn't know if she could chance running again. Not with her son's health at stake. She had a prescription she could refill, but now that Isaiah had found her, did he have the ability to freeze her accounts?

She had to be smart. Which meant she couldn't run without a plan.

Taking a deep breath, she moved into the small room off the living room where she'd set up her office. There was no real door, just an opening where one should have been. For some reason, the people who had built the house had never gotten around to putting one in. Which suited her fine. She could work and still watch her son in the evenings.

The moment she stepped inside the office, his blue eyes flew up and captured her. For a moment, she had the ridiculous feeling of being trapped in a cage. She hid her hands in the pockets of the red vest she wore over her dark shirt and forced her legs to keep working. She stopped three feet from him. He was working on a laptop. It wasn't hers. He must have had it in the bag he'd carried with him.

"Yes, Addison?"

Well, if he was going to call her Addison, she wouldn't call him Mr. Bender. He wasn't her keeper, and she refused to give him the impression that he was in charge. Although, he kind of was.

"I fixed some dinner, Isaiah. You should eat before the police get here."

He grimaced. "I'm in the middle of something. Give me a few minutes?"

She would give him more than that. Without a word, she left. She'd offered him food. If he wanted to eat it cold, that was his business.

Her resolution to let him be lasted until she and Oliver were seated. Her son folded his hands, waiting for her to lead them in prayer.

"Don't forget the man, Mommy. You got to pray for him, too."

The words stuck in her throat. How could she pray for him? But if she didn't, she would be setting a poor example of Christian charity. Not to mention her curious boy would want to know why.

That was not a conversation she wanted to have with him right now.

Keeping her voice low so Isaiah wouldn't hear her, she included him in the prayer.

Content, Ollie shoved a large helping of omelet into his mouth, not fussing at the spinach. When he'd first been diagnosed six months earlier, he'd refused to eat anything green. It had been a daily battle to get him to eat what his body needed to stay strong.

She lifted the first bite of her omelet to her mouth. A twinge of guilt turned it to sawdust on her tongue.

Sighing, she put her fork down. She grabbed the empty plate on the table and placed an omelet and several slices of bacon on it. Rising from her seat, she poured a glass of milk, then gathered the plate in her free hand.

"Darling, I'll be back in a jiffy. I want to give Mr. Isaiah something to eat."

Ollie smiled at her, his own mouth full, and gave her a thumbs up.

She moved briskly to the other room and strode to the desk. Careful not to spill any of the milk on the surface, she placed both the glass and the plate on the desk. The fork slid off the dish with a soft clink. She looked at Isaiah just long enough to catch his startled gaze before swiftly pivoting on her heel and speed walking back to the kitchen.

She sat, her cheeks flushed, and continued eating her meal. Her next bite was perfect, now that she no longer felt guilt stabbing her conscience. Still, she could not eat more than half a dozen bites due to her unsettled stomach.

"Mommy, can I watch my show when I'm done?"

"Yes. Since you didn't have pizza, you can watch an extra episode."

It would keep him occupied. The police were bound to arrive soon. She didn't want him to be a party to that.

She waited until Ollie had cleaned his plate before dumping the remainder of her meal in the trash can. She quickly cleared the table and washed the dishes. Oh! Isaiah still had his plate and the glass of milk. She'd wipe off the table and counter first, then go and retrieve them.

She ignored the voice in her head that called her a coward for procrastinating. She'd be in the bounty hunter's presence soon enough, whether she wanted to be or not.

And she definitely did not.

Isaiah had been deep into his research when Addison set a plate of bacon and eggs with a glass of milk beside him. He was oddly touched by the kindness. When he lifted a forkful of egg to his mouth, he nearly sighed. It had been years since he'd enjoyed a meal he hadn't cooked himself or ordered at a restaurant. He'd intended to eat quickly and continue his work. This rare treat changed his mind. He consumed his meal slowly, enjoying each morsel. The milk was ice cold, just the way he liked it.

It was a simple meal, but one he'd remember.

In the living room, he could hear the television turn on. Soon, the soft sounds of a childish cartoon filtered through the air. Ollie giggled. The infectious sound brought a smile to Isaiah's face.

Setting the plate aside, he turned his attention back to his computer screen.

By this point, doubts were flooding him. So much didn't add up. Her appearance wasn't spot on with the photos he had. The time and location of the crimes she had supposedly committed didn't fit with someone living out in the middle of nowhere with a child. He didn't believe for a moment that Ollie had been abandoned to fend for himself on those occasions. The child was obviously very well cared for and certain of his mother's love.

Add in the complication of diabetes, and there was no way the woman he'd met would leave him unattended for any length of time.

But if she was innocent, why was there a hit on her? That would suggest that she was, on some level, guilty of something. Or would it?

Even if she was not who he'd thought, she might not be completely innocent.

His thoughts were broken when the doorbell rang. Immediately, his hand went to the gun at his waist. He heard Addison call Ollie back to the kitchen. The child whined once, but his mother's stern voice put an end to that. Ollie sighed and stomped back to the kitchen.

The doorbell rang again. Isaiah slipped out of the office, his hand still on his holster. Addison met him in the hallway. Her face was pale but resolute. He gestured for her to stay back. When she nodded and stepped back into the kitchen, he went to the door.

Glancing out, he saw Lieutenant Bartlett and Officer Yates standing on the porch. Relieved, he gave them a signal to wait and re-holstered his weapon before opening the door. The two cops entered the house.

"Addison," Isaiah called out.

Her head peeked around the doorway. When she spotted her guests, the rest of her body flowed around the corner. While her expression wasn't happy to see the two cops standing in her house, some of the tension melted from her shoulders. She strode forward to greet them.

"Ma'am, is there a way we can talk quietly?"

"Give me a moment."

Isaiah locked and bolted the door while she returned to Ollie. A moment later, she walked back into the living room, holding Ollie by the hand.

"Isaiah, I'm going to put a movie on for Ollie. Can you guys wait in the kitchen?"

He grinned. She was bold. She knew he was tracking her, and here she was ordering him and the cops around in her home. She didn't know yet how deep his doubts ran. Briefly, he wondered how spunky she was when death and mayhem weren't penning her in on all sides.

Lieutenant Bartlett and Officer Yates made themselves comfortable at the kitchen table. Isaiah stood in the doorway. Addison settled Ollie in front of the television, with firm directions to remain in the living room. Once she had his promise, she straightened to join the rest of the adults. When their eyes met, he saw the fear in them. Instinct told him this wasn't fear of him or the cops in the other room.

He moved to her side. "What's wrong?"

She shook her head, then shrugged. "I'm being paranoid, maybe. But suddenly I got worried that someone might be upstairs and would come down when we're all in the kitchen."

He slid a hand up her arm. He'd checked the house when they had returned, but if he could ease her mind now, he would. "Wait here."

Moving to the doorway, he relayed her concerns to the cops. Within moments, he and the two officers had checked the entire house and the basement. Only once the place had been established as safe did they move to the kitchen.

Addison stepped close to his side before he sat down. "Thank you."

He should absolutely not be noticing her breath on his ear, or the slight scent like a mixture of sweet coconut and vanilla wafting past his nostrils. He had to stop himself from inhaling deeply to further explore the captivating aromas.

Silently, he claimed a chair at the circular table, placing himself across from Officer Yates, sandwiched between Addison and Lieutenant Bartlett. His back was to the sink. From where he sat, he had an unobstructed view of the front door.

Addison, he noticed, adjusted her chair so she could see her son at all times through the doorway. After today, he approved, remembering how easily his own sister had been taken. The subtle shift brought her closer to his side.

He focused on the interview.

Addison didn't hold back. His eyebrows climbed his forehead several times as the full story unloaded. She'd already told him about the stalker in Pennsylvania. He recalled her saying her husband had been a police officer, but she hadn't gotten around to telling him the whole story about Ollie's father, though he'd read part of that story while she'd been in the kitchen. He let her tell it.

"My husband, Officer William Johnson, was killed four years ago."

"Your husband was William Johnson?" Officer Yates said, shocked. "From Meadville?"

She blinked at the interruption. "Yes."

"I was in the police academy with him. I remember how excited he was when he asked his girlfriend Addie to marry him. I never connected it to you," the rookie said. "I didn't know he'd been killed."

She swallowed and nodded. "Yes. He was out on patrol and someone ambushed him. He was shot in the back of the head."

"The police branded it as a traffic stop that had gone bad," Lieutenant Bartlett said.

Addison nodded. "That's what they told me."

He heard the doubt in her voice. She didn't believe it was a random attack. Interesting.

Isaiah frowned. "If someone is after Addison, maybe her husband's death should be looked into again."

She jerked her head to look at him, shocked. "But he died more than three years before the stalking began."

"It's probably nothing, but it would be best to have all the facts." He was going on pure instinct with this.

Lieutenant Bartlett made some notes without comment. Then she asked another question. The conversation continued for a few more minutes. While Officer Yates seemed to be sympathetic, the lieutenant was harder to read. Several times, she narrowed her eyes during the interview. He turned his attention to Addison.

"I was working as an art teacher when I became pregnant with Oliver. Bill and I had talked about me staying home once we had children, but then he died. Suddenly, staying home wasn't an option, not if I wanted to pay rent and childcare."

Her voice wobbled. She fell silent for a moment, her gaze staring out the windows. They all waited while she regained her composure. "I'm sorry."

"Take your time." The lieutenant reassured her. Although her voice was comforting, Isaiah wasn't fooled. Lieutenant Bartlett hadn't been convinced of her innocence yet. She was one who would require hard evidence and wouldn't be convinced by a sob story, no matter how well it was told.

He respected that. Still, his instincts told him Addie was not the coldhearted, manipulative person they were led to believe.

"I don't know when the stalking started. I

had started to feel like someone was watching me around the time Oliver turned three. When it got bad and I had to move, I decided I needed to disappear. I changed my last name back to Bruce, my maiden name, and I started working as a medical transcriptionist."

"Why not try working as an art teacher again?" Officer Yates queried.

She frowned, tilting her head. "Wouldn't that have been foolish? What if the stalker found my trail and looked up local art teachers? Anyway, there was a benefit to becoming a transcriptionist. I could work from home. Which meant if there was ever an emergency with Ollie, I'd be accessible. And I can meet him every afternoon when he gets off the bus. If I still worked as a teacher, I would have to leave my job the minute the bell rang to meet his bus. The driver won't let him out unless he sees me."

She missed teaching. He could tell that by the way she spoke. But she'd sacrificed her chosen profession for her child.

"What if someone else meets the bus?" If someone else helped with Ollie, that would be a hole in her alibi.

The words confused the officers, but she turned and shot him an icy glare. Clearly, she understood. "I'm the only one authorized to get him."

That was easy to check. If what she said was true, then the last theft she was supposed to have committed couldn't have been her. The time stamp from the ATM machine and her son's bus log would provide her with an alibi.

If her son went to school. He'd have to check his attendance record. By the time the police got up to leave, Isaiah had more questions than answers.

Lieutenant Bartlett pulled him aside. "I remember the story about her husband's death. I also seem to recall his wife disappearing before being charged with larceny and fraud. I'm assuming that's why you're here."

He nodded. He'd wondered if she would connect the dots.

"Don't take your eyes off her," the lieutenant warned him. "She's out of our jurisdiction, and already in your custody, but I won't hesitate to take her in if I feel she's a threat to my town."

He got the message. She wouldn't interfere with his job, but she'd keep an eye on the situation. Obviously, she didn't completely trust him. He was curious about what a seasoned cop would make of the charges. "What's your take on her? Do you think she's guilty of larceny?"

"I don't know. I will be checking into her husband's death closely. It seems a little too pat for me."

The lieutenant suspected Addie of murder? His gut told him she was wrong. Still, his gut wouldn't be able to prove anything. He would need facts.

The lieutenant gave him a level stare and a single nod before she followed Officer Yates out the door.

He sighed. Her skepticism was another complication. At least she wasn't trying to interfere in how he worked. He'd run into pushback from the local law enforcement before. Bounty hunting was a vastly misunderstood field. Many envisioned a vigilante breaking laws left and right, doing anything to get their fugitive. Some felt the field should be outlawed altogether. In fact, it was illegal in Oregon, Kentucky, Wisconsin and Illinois.

Addison was washing dishes with her sleeves pushed up when he noticed she had a long, puckered scar on her left arm, one that ran from the bend in her elbow to the inside of her wrist. It was white with age.

"What happened there?"

She glanced at it. "I almost forgot about this scar. I was in the car crash that killed my parents when I was ten. My arm was broken, and a piece of metal was embedded in my arm. Why?"

"As I already told you, I was contracted to find you and bring you back to Pittsburgh, Pennsylvania, to face charges of identity theft, fraud and vandalism."

"I didn't commit any of those crimes!"

Ignoring her protests, he pulled out his phone and showed her the images of the fugitive he'd been following. She stared at the slender look-alike with dark hair on the screen.

"This is the Addison Johnson I've been contracted to find."

"That's not me!"

"I believe that. The photo's fuzzy enough, though, that it could be. Except for one thing." He pointed to the woman's bare arm. "This woman doesn't have a scar on her arm. And your scar is so thick and rough, it would be very difficult to cosmetically hide it. I don't know who you've angered, or why, but I do know that there is someone else committing crimes in your name. And someone wants you dead."

She stumbled away from him, shaking her head. "No. Why would anyone want me dead? I have not done anything wrong. I don't even speed. Much. I'm a widow with a son. Why? Isaiah, why?"

"I don't know."

Her reaction couldn't be faked. The last bit of doubt cracked and melted away. She was an innocent and so was her son. Just like his sister had been. And Raymond. He shifted his mind away from the two tragedies that had formed his obsession with bringing outlaws to justice.

It had been easier when he'd believed she'd been a criminal. Now, seeing her distress, knowing she was being set up to be taken out, there was no way he could walk away. He couldn't leave her to fend for herself.

Before he could tell her any of this, Ollie screamed from the next room.

FIVE

"Ollie!" Addison raced into the living room, frantic to reach her son. He stood in the middle of the room, pointing at the large picture window half hidden behind the large Christmas tree in the center of the room. Addison scooped him up in her arms. He remained stiff, his attention still focused on the window. She frowned, hugging his shaking body closer. The curtains were drawn. Why was he scared?

"Ollie, what scared you? I don't see anything, honey."

"I saw a man."

She glanced at the thick cloth draping the glass. They were pulled completely shut. "How did you see him?"

"I heard something. I peeked. I'm sorry, Mommy."

She sucked in her breath. They had a rule. Oliver wasn't allowed near the windows when they were closed. Or the doors. If someone knocked, he came and got her. Or if he wanted to look out, the same rule. To some it might seem like overkill. But she'd learned to be cautious.

Isaiah slipped past them and moved near to the window. He glanced at her over his shoulder, jerking his chin slightly. She got the message.

"Honey, let's go into the other room." She took Ollie's hand in hers. He hugged Bowie close to his chest and allowed her to lead him back toward the hallway. She glanced back at the solitary man. "Be careful."

He dipped his head in acknowledgment, then flattened himself against the wall. With one hand, he slowly peeled the fabric an inch from the pane and peered out, twisting his neck and body several times for a better angle. The curtain moved slightly, brushing the back branches of the Christmas tree. A single ornament landed on the plain tree skirt and rolled.

She didn't realize she was holding her breath until he let the heavy curtain drop back into place and straightened, shaking his head.

"Nothing there now." It was all in that one word. *Now.* Meaning he believed there could have been someone there earlier. Or was she reading too much into his simple statement?

"What do you think he saw?" she asked, keeping her tone gentle so her son wouldn't sense her worry. Ollie wasn't one to make up stories. Although, this afternoon had been traumatic enough that anyone's imagination would be working overtime.

His glance flicked to Ollie, still huddled against her side. "I don't know. I am going to check it out. You two stay inside. Lock the door behind me."

He drew a gun from a holster under his shirt. Oliver gasped. Her son had never seen a real gun up close before. She hated that he had seen one now. On the other hand, it helped knowing Isaiah was prepared to defend himself. And them, if needed.

Still, her heart lurched into her throat as he opened the front entrance and slipped outside as silent as a shadow. The door clicked shut behind him. For a moment, she remained where she was, one hand holding tight to Ollie, the other clutching the base of her neck. Her mouth dried like a grape baked in the sun.

"Addie!" Isaiah's voice hissed. "Lock the door."

Releasing Ollie, she motioned for him to remain where he was, then she darted to the door and turned the lock. The mechanism sounded unnaturally loud in the room. Walking backward, she kept her attention trained on where she'd last seen Isaiah and reached behind her, her hand fluttering until Ollie leaped forward to grab it.

They waited.

It could have been five minutes or an hour before she heard a crisp knock. "Addie. It's me. Isaiah."

Running forward, she threw open the door and grabbed hold of his arm, dragging him inside. Slamming the door and re-locking it, she fought the impulse to throw her arms around him. A flush heated her cheeks. Why would she hug the bounty hunter coming after her? Even though she now knew he was on her side, she had only met this man hours ago.

And he had already saved her life once.

She was relieved he was all right, she told herself.

"Did you see him?" Ollie asked. His eyes were wide. But he didn't seem frightened anymore. Rather, his round face shone with excitement. He opened his mouth again. Uh-oh. She knew that look. Isaiah was about to get peppered with a million questions. When Ollie got started, he often launched queries one after another, sometimes not even leaving time for his target to respond.

"Did you see him? The man at the window? What did he want? Is that a real gun? Mommy won't let me have a toy gun. Can't have one at school, neither. Have you ever shot it?"

The corners of Isaiah's lips curled. Shaking his head slightly, he grinned down at Ollie, who was still firing questions at him. When her son stopped to take in a deep breath, Isaiah reached out and put a hand on his shoulder.

"Easy, Oliver. I can't answer that fast. No, I didn't see anyone out there. Yes, I have a real gun, but you can't see it. Guns are dangerous, and only grown-ups who have special training should touch them. I need to talk with your mom for a few minutes, okay?"

Ollie grumbled but allowed Addison to get him a snack. While he was eating, Isaiah beckoned her to come closer. When he spoke, his voice was little more than a husky whisper designed for her ears only.

"I didn't see anyone, but there's evidence that someone was there recently."

"That man said others would be coming for me." She shuddered, remembering Darryl Hughes's harsh voice.

A gentle hand on her shoulder startled her from the dark place her memories had taken her. Blinking, she lifted her chin and stared at him. How strange. Hours ago, he'd been one of the enemies. Now, he was the only one she could trust.

"That's why we've got to plan. You can't stay here. If Darryl found you, there was probably some kind of trail that led him here. Others will follow. I know. That's how I found you."

Her lungs deflated, leaving her unable to catch her breath. His strong, warm hands gripped her shoulders and squeezed. "Take a breath, Addie. You're not alone. Not anymore."

The pressure in her chest eased. She gulped in huge gulps of air. When she felt strong enough, she backed away from him. His arms fell away.

"You were going to turn me in this afternoon."

He nodded, his brow furrowed. "Yeah, I was. But then I actually met you and realized you couldn't possibly be the person I was contracted to find. However, we're going to have to find out the truth to clear your name. Otherwise, if I don't bring you back, they might send someone else after you."

Great. She'd started to feel safe. Only to find there were people who wanted her either dead or in jail for crimes she hadn't committed. Well, at least Isaiah believed her. For now. She would trust him for the time being. But she would remain on her guard just in case he changed his mind about her.

"What do we do now?"

He leaned to the left, scanning the room, no doubt for little ears, then straightened and faced her again. "I left my car parked halfway between here and Tricia's house. We're going to need it. While I go and retrieve it, I think you ought to pack."

Her heart sank. She had known it was coming, so she kept silent and nodded.

"How much should I pack, do you think?"

"Whatever you think is absolutely necessary. No frills. If you don't need it, then it stays behind. And Addie—" his hand touched her shoulder "—you should plan on not returning for the foreseeable future."

She swallowed her protests. It made sense. They didn't have any idea where they were going or for how long. She'd pack clothes, food, Ollie's diabetic supplies. But she'd allow for two "frills." Ollie's dog, whom he never parted with, and her Bible.

She didn't know what Isaiah's position on faith was. What she did know was that without God on her side, she and her son would never survive. He was all that had kept her going up till now. Which meant she was willing to risk Isaiah's disapproval in this one instance.

"Here." She strode to the bowl on the kitchen counter and grabbed her spare house key. "I will lock the door. Take this key so you can let yourself in when you're back."

"You should also give me your cell phone number in case I need help, or in case you need my help."

She nodded and they exchanged phone numbers. She never thought she'd see the day when she would have a bounty hunter listed as one of her contacts. If the situation weren't so dire, it would've been funny. Something she would've shared with a friend, if she had any of those. However, the one and only friend she had made in the past six months was dead, killed by a man who had been coming after Addie.

She blocked the guilt creeping in, whispering that Tricia's death was her fault. She'd done nothing to deserve what was happening.

Isaiah tapped his number into her phone then handed it back to her with a single nod.

In the short time she had known him, she had gotten used to the lack of expression on his face. He reminded her of a character she once saw on a science fiction television show who didn't show emotion. But then she caught his gaze again. There was a wealth of feeling in those blue eyes.

He broke their connection and turned to complete his mission.

Her insides quivered as he once again slipped out into the night. She said a quick prayer for his safe return.

Then she turned back to the kitchen and started gathering the items they would need. Thankfully, she had refilled Oliver's insulin prescription two days ago. Which meant she had enough to get him by for a while. She just needed to make sure it was kept refrigerated. A quiet snort left her. That shouldn't be too difficult. After all, it was the middle of December in Ohio. She could probably just leave it in the trunk, and it would stay plenty cold. She grabbed the small ice chest she kept for his extra medicine and filled it with the ice packs from the freezer.

Setting the filled ice chest aside, she turned around to go back to the bedroom and begin packing.

Her eyes landed on a large man moving in front of her two seconds before his hands closed around her throat.

Isaiah parked his car in front of the garage and shut off the ignition. He shoved the door open. An arctic blast hit him in the face and nipped past his collar, zinging down his back. He shivered. He should have known better than to go out with his coat unzipped. That was what he got for being in a hurry.

Exiting the vehicle, he grabbed the backpack he'd had stowed in the car. Then he hit the remote lock and shoved his hands into his pockets. He hadn't taken more than three steps from the car when his phone vibrated. Regretfully, he took his right hand out of the warmth of his coat to grab his phone. It was Officer Yates. He made a split decision to answer the call out of the house.

"Isaiah Bender," he said into the phone.

"Good evening, Isaiah. Alan Yates here. I have some information I thought you would want."

"Go ahead. I'm listening."

Yates cleared his throat on the other end of the phone. Isaiah could almost see him sticking his fingers under his collar to loosen it. The guy's nervousness came through even when he wasn't talking face-to-face.

"So, I have a source that I go to for information. According to this person, Addison Johnson does in fact have a price on her head. It specifically states that it is a $50,000 reward for her body. We still can't see who put up the reward. It's one of those things that goes out on the internet and all sorts of creeps come out of the woodwork to claim the prize."

Isaiah figured that was the case. "Do me a favor? Let me know if you find out who wants her dead? I'm curious to know if it's connected to the warrants for her arrest." Lieutenant Bartlett already knew why he was with Addie. He didn't know how convinced she was of Addie's guilt. Her response before she'd left earlier hadn't been clear.

Isaiah wondered how far could he trust the cops to help him get her safe? If they believed she was a fugitive, they would protect her, but they would also have a duty to hand her over to the precinct in Pennsylvania. It was possible that they would not interfere. After all, the crimes were committed in another jurisdiction, and he already technically had her in his custody. Still, it would be nice to know exactly where they stood with the Sutter Springs Police Department.

"Will do. I've got to tell you, I can't see her being involved in identity theft or any of those crimes. The woman I saw today was concerned with one thing—protecting that little boy. She was absolutely shocked by her friend's murder."

Isaiah hummed. A noncommittal response was best.

Yates laughed once. "What do I know, right? Maybe I haven't seen as much as you or some of the veteran cops. But that's my gut instinct."

"I always trust my instincts," Isaiah admitted. Right now, those instincts were screaming at him to end the call and get inside the house. He headed to the front door.

Inside, Oliver was shrieking. A continuous scream of terror.

"Yates!" he yelled. "Something's happening in the house. I need the cops here."

"On our way!"

He hung up and ran the rest of the way to the door. Shoving his hand into his pocket for the extra key, he realized he had left it sitting in the console area of his car. He didn't have time to go back and retrieve it. Addie and Ollie needed him now. Charging at the door, he used his shoulder as a battering ram. Something cracked, but the lock held tight. Backing up, he made another run for it. This time, the wood splintered and the doorknob rolled out of its socket. The impact slammed through his entire body. Even his teeth hurt. He ignored his aching teeth and his aching jaw.

Kicking the doorknob and splintered wood aside with his boots, he rushed to the kitchen. Addie was fighting for her life, her hands helplessly scratching and tearing at her assailant's wrists. The man was too large for her to have any effect.

Isaiah attacked the man, ripping him away from Addie. The two men fell to the ground.

Unlike in his tussle with Darryl, Addie's current attacker equaled Isaiah in skill. They rolled again. This time the stranger had the advantage.

Lying flat on the floor, Isaiah struggled to regain his footing. Over the other man's shoulder, he saw movement. Addie had a large, cast iron skillet in her hand. Isaiah stopped struggling. She wound up the dish like a bat and smacked the side of the attacker's head with it, grunting when it struck him.

The man slumped to the side and collapsed on the clean floor in a boneless heap. Isaiah yanked his legs free and stood, brushing off his hands on his pants.

The skillet dropped from Addie's fingers and clanged to the floor.

"Mommy!" Ollie crashed into her legs. She wobbled.

Isaiah pushed her into a chair before she fell. "Are you all right?"

She nodded, tears in her eyes. Already, bruises were darkening the delicate skin at her throat. Isaiah fought down a wave of rage rising inside him like a hurricane. He needed to remain steady and clearheaded. Addie and Ollie came first. He forced the anger aside.

"I have to tie him up in case he awakens."

He left her long enough to grab the zip ties from his backpack. He had another set of handcuffs in his car, but he hesitated to leave Addie and Ollie alone in the house with the assailant. Besides, Darryl Hughes had destroyed his good set of cuffs. This guy would demolish his old ones in no time.

It was time to update his equipment. After he got Addie and Ollie to safety.

"Police!"

"Back here! In the kitchen!" Isaiah shouted.

Officer Yates and Lieutenant Bartlett barreled into the small area. They halted, jaws dropping, at the scene that met them.

The lieutenant began to question Addie.

Isaiah interrupted her. "This man attempted to strangle her. I think she needs to be checked at the hospital, make sure there's no damage, before she answers any more questions."

Addie began shaking her head, pointing to her son.

Isaiah scooted a chair next to her and sat, his knees touching hers. "I know you are worried about Ollie. I won't leave him—or you—but we need to make sure you're not injured."

"I'm fine," she whispered.

"Mommy." Ollie climbed into her lap. Her arms pulled him snug against her. He settled in his head on her shoulder. "Mommy, the doctor will make you feel better. Just like you tell me."

Isaiah bit back a sudden grin. It wasn't the place for humor. She'd nearly been killed. But that kid was smart as a whip. He didn't know if he was intentionally manipulating his mom, but he had a feeling little Oliver Bruce knew exactly what he was about.

He made a decision. "I will take them both to the hospital while you deal with the mess here." He jerked his thumb at the man on floor, who was beginning to stir and moan.

Lieutenant Bartlett nodded. "We'll be in touch."

He didn't wait around to hear more. Ushering Ollie and Addie out the door, he loaded their bags and the cooler with Ollie's medication into his trunk. Then he hopped into the car and revved the engine, backing out of the driveway as fast as he could while still being a safe driver. He pulled away and headed toward the hospital, his eyes roving to locate any lurking dangers.

A light on his dashboard lit up, indicating he had a Bluetooth call coming through. He reached out a hand to answer the call, then halted, his fingers curling up into a fist.

"You're not going to answer that?" Addie's soft voice asked. He tilted his head enough to see her face, dimly lit up by the lights on the console. Outside, the night sky was inky black, contrasting with the glitter of the snow when the headlights hit it.

He shook his head. "I know that number. It's the person who put up the bond for you. I can't help but wonder if this is all connected. The killers finding you at the same time I did."

"It might be a coincidence."

He snorted. "I highly doubt it. And even if it is, so what? I can hardly hand you over, not when I know you're innocent."

SIX

Addie hadn't realized how much it meant to her that he believed her to be innocent.

She swallowed the emotion clogging her throat. It had been a long time since she had anyone else besides herself to rely on. *Don't get used to having him around*, she warned herself sternly. *As soon as his part is cleared up, he'll be gone.*

Then it would be her and Ollie on their own again.

And God. Her lids swept closed for a brief moment while she sent up a silent prayer, thanking God for His protection and asking Him to continue watching over them. She started to open her eyes, then paused.

And Lord, please be with Isaiah. I don't know what trauma he's been through, but I think something bad happened to him. I don't

*know if he's a praying man, so I'm interced-
ing on his behalf.*

"Praying?"

She opened her eyes and turned to see the
man silhouetted beside her. "Always."

If she'd hoped his question would open a
discussion on the merits of faith and prayer,
she was disappointed. He grunted, his attention on the snowy road ahead.

After five minutes of awkward silence, she
cleared her throat. "I'm glad you believe I'm
innocent. What I'm worried about is proving
it."

"That might not be as difficult as you think."
Isaiah picked up his phone from where it rested
in the cup holder. He handed it to her. "Here."

She took the phone gingerly, almost as if she
was afraid it would bite her. "You want me to
use your phone?"

He nodded. "Yes, ma'am." He rattled off the
passcode to unlock the device. "Go into my
work apps. Find the one for notes."

She unlocked the phone and swiped through
until she found the correct app. She tapped it
and waited for it to open. Looking at the vari-
ous files, she saw they were all tagged with
funny names.

"Which file am I looking for?"

He didn't answer at first. "Umm. Okay, so I had to name these something that wouldn't give away your identity."

"Are all of these your fugitives?"

He shook his head. "Once a case is done, I delete the information from my phone. I have it saved elsewhere."

She nodded. "I'm opening…?"

"Open the one that says, 'She has a great smile.'"

She blinked. He thought she had a great smile? She understood why he was acting embarrassed, but her quirky sense of humor was amused. She tapped the file. It opened up and the first thing she saw were pictures of her from before she'd run.

Immediately following were the shots of the look-alike using a stylus to take money from ATMs. "I'll bet she used a stylus so there wouldn't be any fingerprints," she mused.

"That's my guess."

She stared at the images. They were grainy, but she could see the resemblance. "Her face is a touch longer than mine."

"Yeah. I noticed that. In the one picture, you can also see her dark eyes. Of course, contacts could have been used to change the eye color."

"And here's the one you showed me earlier without the scar."

"She used your name. The car she drives away in is registered to Addison Johnson, with all your information. So, she really did steal your identity."

She had never felt so violated. Someone was out there in the world committing crimes under her name.

"Scroll down. I have a list of the crime dates. I think our best bet to clear your name is to have a solid alibi for as many of those dates as possible. You're smart, but even you can't be in two places at once."

"True. Bilocation is not in my wheelhouse." She did as he said and scrolled through until one of the days listed jumped out at her. "Here. This one on September 18. I couldn't possibly have been in New York."

She shivered, remembering the day in question. Isaiah turned up the heat. Warm air whooshed out of the vents. She nodded. "Thanks."

"What happened that day?"

He had to know if he was going to help her. She flicked a glance to the backseat to make sure Ollie wasn't listening in.

"Ollie had a new preschool teacher. The

other one had quit suddenly. Anyway, she lost track of time and skipped snack. When she realized it, she decided not to bother with it because she didn't want to wreak havoc on the rest of her schedule. I got an alert on my phone that Ollie was having a low-glucose event. The teacher thought he was tired and put him in a corner to sleep it off."

She fisted her hands in her lap. "I met the paramedics at the door. Ollie's glucose levels were dangerously low. We went to the emergency room to get him checked out and were there for over four hours."

"That's awful," he ground out. Anger rumbled in his deep voice. "Please tell me you didn't send him back."

"As if any mother would. No. I withdrew him the next day, and the following week he started going to the preschool program at Sutter Springs Elementary School."

"You'll have medical documentation for that day. I think that should be enough to cause reasonable doubt and clear your name. Any of the other days?"

She looked them over then pointed to one of them. "Here. The days in July? My husband's paternal grandmother had gotten in touch with us. I'd never met her before. My husband had never met her. He'd been estranged from that side of his family for most of his life. She wanted to meet me and Oliver. We spent the weekend in Seattle."

"That will do it. If she can corroborate those dates, you'll be in the clear."

Sighing, she leaned back in her seat, some of the tension leaving her. "I wish we could get that price taken off my head."

"I won't leave you alone. We'll get through this. I promise."

He didn't seem like the kind of man to make idle promises. She had the feeling that once Isaiah Bender gave his word, he kept it, no matter what.

He took her to the hospital, as planned. The lieutenant had called ahead, ensuring that she was on the priority list to see the doctor on call. As a result, when they arrived, there was only one patient ahead of her. They were in and out of there in under an hour. Oliver conked out while they waited for the doctor to release Addie.

"I would have never believed it possible to spend less than three hours in the ER." Isaiah commented as they left the emergency room. He hefted Oliver a little higher in his arms. The child let out a soft snore and nestled in closer. She grinned. He'd sleep through any-thing.

"What now?"

Isaiah opened his mouth to answer, but a yawn slipped out. "I think we should get some rest in the motel I have booked. I need to make some calls and plan our next move. If your pic-ture is all over the net, we need to take some precautions."

She was too tired to argue. He drove them to the one-story motel off the interstate. By-passing the lobby carport, he drove along the line of connected rooms and parked in front of room 117. She'd never felt completely safe in motels with exits on the outside. Pressing her lips together, she picked up her exhausted son and followed Isaiah to the door. He let her in and gestured to the bed farthest from the door.

"I'll get the rest of the stuff from the trunk."

She watched him leave then turned to get her son to bed.

She set Ollie on his feet briefly. He muttered and leaned all his weight against her. She held him upright with one arm and used the other one to pull back the covers. He climbed in and let her remove his shoes, then promptly fell over and curled himself into a ball, like a cat. She covered him up and sat in one of the two chairs in the room, determined to wait for Isaiah. Weariness settled over her like a heavy weighted blanket. She rubbed her eyes. They felt like sandpaper.

Isaiah entered. He locked and bolted the door before setting a large camo duffel bag on the lone table. It clanked. She sat straight up and leaned forward, interested in spite of her growing need for sleep.

"What do you have in there? The kitchen sink?"

His lips tipped up in a small smile. He took out a small key and unlocked the tiny lock before he opened the bag and waved at it. "Just the tools of the trade."

Peering in, she shivered. Isaiah didn't only travel with the gun on his belt.

He had an arsenal.

Isaiah glanced behind him to make sure that Oliver was truly asleep. He never left weapons out where a child could get to them. However, after the day they'd experienced, he couldn't leave his bag in the car. If someone broke into the room, he would be ready.

One by one, he lifted his tools out. He set his laptop on the bedside table and plugged it into the charger. He checked his best bullet-proof vest. He hadn't worn it for a few days. Even though he'd bought it two years ago, it was like new. He had an older pair of handcuffs. Hopefully, they would work better than the other ones. He lifted out the pepper spray and handed it to Addie.

"Why don't you carry this? It might come in handy."

She accepted it, reluctance stamped on her face, and shoved it into her backpack. "I really hope I won't need it. But thanks."

"Anytime." He returned to his bag. His Taser was there. He might want to carry that when they left. He set it beside the computer. Then he sealed up the bag again and fastened the lock. Rather than leaving the duffel bag out in the open where a curious four-year-old might be tempted to poke it and explore, he shoved it against the wall and covered it with a blanket before taking the wooden chair from beside the table and setting it over the bag to block it from view.

Since he wore the key on the chain around his neck, he wasn't afraid that Ollie would be able to open it. Sighing, he lifted his arms above his head and stretched, half turning to survey the room. He grinned when his gaze landed on Addie. She'd fallen asleep sitting in the chair.

Should he wake her? He didn't want her to get a crink in her neck. However, he didn't want to disturb her, knowing she needed her rest. And some people had trouble falling back to sleep once they woke up. He didn't know her well enough to know if she fit into that category.

No. He'd allow her to sleep in peace. Although, it was still a little chilly in the room. It wasn't a fancy hotel. He stood in front of the window and grimaced at the cold draft coming through. He couldn't fix that.

Moving to the thermostat, he tried to increase the heat output. When the blower hadn't kicked on five minutes later, he sighed. This was as good as it was going to get, he acknowledged.

He dragged back the comforter on his bed and let it fall to the floor. He never used the top layer. He yanked off the second blanket. It was thinner but made of heavier material. Plus, it was fuzzy. He also took one of the four pillows from the bed. Who needed four pillows, anyway? Carrying them over to Addie, he gently placed the pillow in the space between her head and the wall. Then he wrapped the blanket around her, moving as slowly as he could so she wouldn't awaken. She sighed in her sleep and snuggled down, shifting so her head rested on the pillow.

That was the best he could do in the circumstances.

He went to the bathroom and splashed cold water on his face. All he wanted to do was climb in bed and sleep. He had been up for twenty-two hours straight, and his body needed to rest. He couldn't give in until he made some phone calls.

Addie's and Ollie's lives depended upon it.

His first call was to Officer Yates. Yates picked up on the second ring.

"Hey, Isaiah. Glad you called. That perp who tried to strangle Addison has a massive rap sheet. No idea how he was still on the streets. Someone needs to lose their job over that one."

"I'm assuming he was after the reward money?"

"You assumed right. The best we can figure, the reward was first posted about four months ago."

"That was only a month after I was hired to find her."

His internal alarm went crazy. This had to be connected.

"I know it. Listen, I know you don't think she did those crimes she's accused of..."

"She didn't. She has alibis for at least two of those dates." He related to Yates what he'd learned in the car.

"Those should be easy enough to check into. Do you remember her husband's grandmother's name?"

"She didn't mention it, but her surname was probably Johnson."

"Like there won't be a million Johnsons in the Seattle area."

Isaiah grinned. "You're not wrong."

Yates was beginning to grow on him. He might be young and inexperienced, but he was sharp and enthusiastic. Good traits to have in law enforcement.

"Look, you protect those two. I will confirm these alibis. We'll continue looking into the reward and keeping watch here. We're a small department, so if we don't have to expend the manpower to guard someone, this case might get solved faster."

He understood. He hung up with the officer and immediately dialed one of his old former military friends.

"Henry. I could use some assistance," he said by way of greeting.

"Isaiah, my man! You got it! Anything you need, let me know."

It was the response he expected. His unit had been close, but he'd been especially close with Henry, Nolan and Zack. Nolan had died two weeks before his tour was up. But he kept in contact with Henry and Zack. In fact, he and Henry often worked cases together.

He explained what he needed without going into too many extra details. Henry didn't need to know who Addie was or why they were on the run. Nor would he ever ask. The friends trusted each other without question and respected the other's privacy.

Once he hung up, he set his alarm and lay down on the bed. He'd sleep for a few hours, then get up before Henry called back in the morning.

Closing his eyes, he wrestled with his mind for a few minutes. His brain wouldn't shut down. Worry for the two people in his care surged through his blood, carried like a swift current.

He recalled Addie in the car. Her voice had been so peaceful after she'd prayed, despite the attacks.

God. I haven't talked to You in a long time. I need help, though. It's not important what happens to me. Please get Addie and Ollie out of this alive.

* * *

Isaiah was already awake and moving around the motel room when she opened her eyes. Addie stretched. A pain shot through her neck. Wincing, she rubbed the aching muscles.

"Good morning." Isaiah sent her a smile before returning to his computer screen.

"Good morning. I can't believe I fell asleep in a chair. I must have been tired." She rubbed her neck again.

"Should I have woken you up?" His brow furrowed.

"No. I'm glad you let me rest. Ollie kicks in his sleep. Oh, and thanks for the pillow and blanket. I wouldn't have slept so well without them."

Ruddy color shaded his cheeks. His jawline sported a five o'clock shadow. He hadn't shaved. It probably wasn't a priority in the current situation.

He looked rugged. Her heartbeat tripped. She spun away from him, hiding her own sudden blush under the guise of checking on Ollie.

Speaking of Ollie. "I need to feed him, and he needs his insulin."

He nodded. "There's a diner down the street. Let's go over there to eat. I have a buddy we need to meet at ten this morning."

She woke up Ollie. "Come on, Olli-gator. Rise and shine. We're going to go get breakfast with Mr. Isaiah."

In typical Ollie fashion, he bolted upright wide awake. She smothered a smile. Her sweet boy had two modes. Sleeping like a hibernating bear or up and running like the Energizer Bunny. There was no middle ground. Encouraging him to hurry, she got him into the bathroom to work on getting him clean and dressed.

Easier said than done. Her squirmy child wouldn't stop talking long enough to brush his teeth and wash his face without threats that Bowie would be put into time-out. That worked. For some odd reason, he didn't care if he was put in time-out. But if she put his stuffed dog in time-out, he acted like his world was coming to an end.

Twenty-five minutes later, she presented a very excited and hungry Oliver, complete with his ever-present stuffed dog, and herself to Isaiah. She'd pinned her hair up and donned a baseball cap. She also wore her reading glasses. It wasn't much of a cover, but hopefully people wouldn't look too closely at her. "We're ready to eat."

Isaiah grinned at the announcement. When

Ollie's stomach rumbled, Isaiah broke into a laugh that seemed to slam into the middle of her chest.

Addie stopped breathing for a moment. The sheer exuberance of that warm, rich laugh, somewhat rusty as if he didn't laugh often, washed over her. It was a sound she'd love to hear again and again.

Shaking herself out of her silly mood, she swiftly collected what they needed and shoved it into her backpack. The small ice chest wasn't convenient, but she'd carry it along anyway. Isaiah shoved his computer and the Taser into a backpack.

"Just in case we need them."

He made them wait until he'd looked outside. Once he declared it was safe, they left the room. Isaiah threw his duffel bag into the trunk of his car. Then he took the ice chest from her.

"Hold my hand, Ollie." She sighed when he slipped his small hand in hers. Lately, he'd been on this kick where he wanted to be a big boy. And big boys didn't hold their mommy's hands when walking. She was glad not to have to fight that battle this morning.

Isaiah opened the diner door for them. It squeaked in protest. Addie ducked her head to avoid notice. Fortunately, they were the only patrons in the small diner. The woman behind the counter hollered for them to seat themselves.

Isaiah chose a booth close to the emergency exit. He sat himself in the bench facing the room, his back to the wall. Ollie and Addie slid into the one opposite him.

The server shuffled over to take their drink orders. Addie took the children's menu before the woman could hand it to Ollie. She smiled at her, ignoring the woman's surprise. Instinct kept her from revealing his disease. Anyone looking for her might know of his condition. It was something the woman would remember.

Addie discreetly administered his insulin, then ordered for them both, avoiding sweet foods heavy on carbs such as pancakes and waffles. Ollie liked eggs and fruit. She ordered the same thing for both of them so he wouldn't feel left out.

Isaiah waited until she had placed their orders. "I'll have the same."

Addie smiled at him. "Thanks," she mouthed, knowing he'd chosen his breakfast with Ollie in mind, too.

He winked at her. She chuckled and shook her head.

Ollie kept up a steady stream of chatter while they ate. She had to remind him twice to eat with his mouth shut. "We don't want to see your food after it leaves your plate."

Isaiah laughed softly. The patience he showed her son amazed her. He would make a good father. Something stopped her from sharing that insight. It was too personal. And while he was patient and kind, Isaiah's manners didn't invite personal commentary.

The server cleared their plates and left the check. Isaiah took some bills from his wallet and paid it, leaving a generous tip. "From here on out, we're going to use only cash. No credit or debit cards. Nothing that can be traced. We'll collect our things from the motel and leave as soon as we possibly can."

She nodded, her nerves tingling and jumpy.

"You're holding too tight, Mommy."

"Sorry, baby." She loosened her death grip on his gloved fingers.

They began to walk back to the motel. The snow crunched beneath their boots and their breath puffed in front of their faces.

"Stop."

At Isaiah's urgent warning, she froze. A midsize car slowly drove through the motel parking lot. It paused behind Isaiah's car.

"Get down."

They huddled behind the line of shrubs on the edge of the property. She didn't question his direction. Ollie pressed his face into her. She held him to her. Through the thinned-out branches, she saw the passenger car door open. A man stepped out, tugged at something, then threw something that was roughly the shape of a football through the window of their room. Glass shattered.

He'd thrown a grenade.

The man jumped back into the car, and the vehicle raced off, tires squealing.

The grenade detonated, obliterating room 117.

If they hadn't left to eat breakfast, all three of them would be dead.

SEVEN

Isaiah launched himself sideways in an attempt to shield both Addie and Ollie. Debris rained down on the parking lot, showering the new snow with dust, shards of wood, plastic and glass. The room he'd rented was a gaping hole with flames consuming what was left of the interior.

When the dust cleared, he straightened, assisting Addie to her feet since Ollie was clutched tightly to her. "We need to stay hidden in case he comes back."

Together, they turned to view the destruction. Even looking through the bushes, it was horrific.

The motel room door had slammed into his car, demolishing the front window. Two of the tires were flat, as if they had melted from the heat. Either that or the flying glass had shredded them.

Business owners and other motel guests congregated in the parking lot, shocked. Isaiah snapped a picture with his phone and sent it to Officer Yates with a text that they were unharmed.

Sirens screamed in the distance. He heard the high-pitched wail of the police or an ambulance. Thirty seconds later, a firetruck blared its horn. Ollie covered his ears. The emergency vehicles converged on the street,

"Why did they leave?" Addie breathed next to him. "Wouldn't they have to prove I was dead to collect the reward?"

"I don't know. They must have a plan. Maybe they've bribed someone, or maybe they're watching the crime scene."

His phone vibrated. It was Henry. "Yeah, Henry."

"Are you okay?"

"We're fine."

"Look, buddy, I just heard that some cop was gunned down near you. An Officer Yates. You know him?"

For a moment, he couldn't see. Instead of Alan Yates's young face, he saw that of Raymond King, his best friend as a child, killed in a hunting accident. A death that could have been prevented. Someone touched his shoulder. Addie. He held up a hand, telling her to wait.

"What happened?"

"He was shot in the back. An eyewitness said it was a woman wanted for several crimes. Allison or Amanda or something."

"Addison," he breathed without thinking.

"Yeah, that's the name. Listen, they think she's with you. The police are everywhere looking for you. He's in the hospital in critical condition."

A cold sweat beaded under his collar. The men coming after Addie knew she was under his protection. Would the police even listen to him now, when one of their own had been nearly killed? He had to get Addie to a safe place so they could think and plan. If they could figure out who was coming after them, who had put a price on her head, maybe they could go to the police.

"Meet me in your hunting cabin at ten. Come alone." He hung up and turned to Addie. Her pale skin and the lines carved next to her mouth told him she knew the news was bad.

"Someone shot Alan Yates. He's not dead, but I don't think he was able to do anything with the information I gave him." She gasped. He had to get it all out before grief took over.

"Addie, they think you and I did it. We have to hide. There are too many obstacles. I don't know if I can trust the police right now."

"Your car—"

"My car is completely out of the question. Not only is it undrivable, but it's sitting in an active crime scene."

Her head jerked up. "My car is at the mechanics, but it's ready. We'll have to walk a mile to get it."

"Will they be open on a Saturday?"

She shook her head. "It doesn't matter. The keys are under the floor mat."

It was the best option they had. "Let's go."

Walking a mile is easy when one is alone. Mix in frigid temperatures, blowing snow hitting your cheeks and nose until you can't feel them anymore, it becomes more difficult. When you add a cranky four-year-old, though, the level of difficulty rises dramatically, making every step an accomplishment.

Not that Ollie was bad, Isaiah mused. For the first twenty minutes, he marched along with them like a real trouper, his little legs doing knee-highs to keep moving in and out of the snow. They couldn't travel as fast as they would if he weren't with them, but that was to be expected.

Twenty-five minutes in, he yanked his hand from Addie's, crossed his arms over his tiny chest and pushed his lower lip out.

"I'm done," he announced. "Ain't going to walk no more."

Isaiah kept his jaw shut, but his eyes widened. He watched Addie. She calmly lifted his stuffed dog in her arms. "Well, if you're sure. Bowie and I are going to keep going."

She started walking away. Isaiah frowned, tempted to call her back. But three seconds later, Ollie yelled and ran after his mom, taking her hand again.

The victory lasted seven minutes.

"Ollie, why don't I give my backpack to your mom, and you can hop on my back?"

Ollie was delighted with the idea. And it worked. But traveling uphill with a wiggly child who talked nonstop was still a challenge.

Oddly enough, Isaiah found he didn't mind so much. Oliver was an energetic boy, but he was also one filled with laughter and curiosity. He reminded Isaiah of his brother Gideon. His memories ached. Gideon was twenty-nine now. He hadn't seen his baby brother since he was fourteen. Was he married?

Were any of his brothers married? Maybe all of them were.

That brought his mind to his parents. Were they both alive? He'd never allowed himself to wonder about them, but suddenly, the ache in his heart yearned to go home. Not to the Amish life. He'd seen and done too much to return to the Amish way of life. But to see his family and tell them he was sorry for leaving without explaining what had happened.

One day, he promised himself. Someday soon he'd go back and tell them why he had left and ask their forgiveness. He'd never been baptized, so maybe they'd let him into the family again, at least on the fringes.

"There it is."

Nearly an hour after they started walking, they reached the mechanic. Isaiah watched as Addie left a check in the box.

"That will alert the police that we have the car."

"Not until Monday morning," she said. She opened the car door and retrieved the keys. "He doesn't open on the weekends. The next time he'll be here is seven-thirty Monday morning. Do you want to drive?"

He shook his head. "It's your car. I don't care if you drive."

"Well, I appreciate that. It's very enlightened of you. But I would prefer you drive. I tend to be overly cautious in the snow, and I wouldn't know how to drive evasively if someone followed us."

"Good point. Hand the keys over."

Addie handed Isaiah the car keys, shivering when his fingers brushed her palm. Flushing, she grabbed the gloves she'd stuffed in her pocket while she wrote the check. Her hands were not cold, though. Where they had come into contact with Isaiah's skin, they tingled with warmth. Like an electric shock.

She buckled Oliver in and then sank into the front passenger seat. Tempted to avoid his gaze, she scoffed at her absurdity. They were in a jam, they needed to be able to look at each other and communicate.

It wasn't like she was falling in love with him. No way. She couldn't afford that. Sure. He was handsome and sweet. But she had a child to raise and a host of people coming out of the woodwork to kill her. There was no place for romance in her life. Plus, she'd been in love before. When Bill had been killed, it had nearly destroyed her. Only her faith and Ollie had pulled her through. She didn't know if she could ever open her heart to that kind of pain again.

She blew out an aggravated breath and leaned her head against the cold window. When did life become so complicated? One day she was a young wife and mother with no worries beyond her family, and the next she was running for her life.

"You okay?" Isaiah's deep voice intercepted her litany of woes.

She gave a bitter chuckle. "Yeah. Just feeling sorry for myself. Pretty pitiful, right?"

He shrugged. "You have a right to be upset and to feel down. To be honest, I'm impressed with how level-headed you are. You've been attacked, nearly strangled, and someone tried to blow you up."

"Don't forget the part about being caught by a bounty hunter."

He chuckled. "That, too. My point is, you haven't lost your cool yet."

"I did when we found Tricia." Her voice was a low growl.

He sighed. "She was a friend. That's different. It hurts when friends get hurt. Even worse than if it were us."

He wasn't wrong. There was a wealth of experience in his heavy tone. "Isaiah?"

"Huh?"

She couldn't do it. No matter how curious she was, she couldn't pry into his life. His pain was his own, and if she was right, it was deep. If she dug too deep, she could tear open wounds that weren't any of her business. He'd been kind to them. She wouldn't repay him by being nosy.

"It's almost nine." She noted to turn the topic. "What time are we meeting your friend?"

He didn't answer her immediately. She shifted to get a better look at his expression. He kept looking into the rearview mirror. His fingers flexed on the wheel.

"Hold on." Without warning, he spun it, steering the vehicle onto a side road. She bit back a cry, bracing herself against the door. Ollie wailed in his booster seat.

She ducked to see into the side mirror. A car was behind them, going too fast for the rough road and the snowy conditions.

"They're following us, aren't they?"

"Yep. I hoped they wouldn't be able to make the turn." He glanced back again. "Ollie, the car will go really fast, and it might seem scary, but I want you to trust me. Okay?"

"Okay." The little boy said in a tiny voice. He had Bowie in a vice grip. She could see the fear on his face, but he wasn't crying.

Her stomach muscles in knots, Addie steeled herself for a rough ride.

He didn't disappoint. Isaiah depressed the gas pedal. The engine roared, and the small car went flying over the gravel road, bouncing over potholes. Their shadow kept up with them. Isaiah hit a curve without decelerating. The back end fishtailed. Addie bit down on her knuckles. Ollie whimpered behind her. While she wanted to reach back and take his hand, she knew it was too dangerous. One solid thump and she would pull his arm, possibly hurting him.

"We're going to take the next right," Isaiah informed her. "I'm going to wait until the last second, though. It will be a hard turn. I'm hoping they'll have trouble with it."

Addie was incapable of responding beyond a single nod. When she saw the road looming ahead of them, she squeezed her eyes shut and prayed with all her might. The car swerved so hard, it almost felt like they were on a roller coaster. For a second, she could swear they went airborne before the tires hit the road again.

Glancing back, she watched their pursuers swing wide to take the curve. Their vehicle continued spiraling after the curve, careening across the road and smashing against a tree.

"They won't be able to back up," Isaiah said. "Both front tires are off the road."

Sighing, she sagged against the seat. "Ollie?"

"I didn't like that, Mommy."

She grinned. "I didn't either, baby, but we're fine. Thanks to Mr. Isaiah's fancy driving."

He grunted. "Glad you two aren't hurt. We'll be to Henry's in about fifteen minutes."

They could hold out that long. "We'll need to get someone a snack and their insulin while we're there."

"We will."

Isaiah's friend Henry was standing outside the most adorable hunting cabin when they drove up. Isaiah put the car in Park and went to the back of the car to get the bag with Ollie's insulin.

Addie checked the monitor on her phone. Ollie's levels were stable. Which was surprising considering the morning they had survived. Stress can negatively impact blood glucose levels. And they had certainly had that.

"Henry Fisher." The man introduced himself.

"Addie. And this is Ollie." She deliberately left off her last name. Although how many Addies were traveling with a four-year-old named Oliver? Probably not that many.

"Henry, while we talk, Addie needs to feed Ollie."

"Sure, no problem. They can do that at the kitchen table. Help yourself to anything in the fridge."

She smiled at his open face, so different from the closed expression that Isaiah showed the world. "Thanks. But we have some food."

She and Ollie went into the house. The men stayed outside, conversing softly. Their deep voices were little more than a rumble, reminiscent of distant thunder before a storm.

Ollie had been fed and she'd snatched an apple for herself by the time the men entered the room. She waited for Isaiah to explain why they needed to come here, to this house in the middle of nowhere.

"Here's the deal," Isaiah began. "We can't stay in the area. I don't know if the police are going to be searching for us, but with Officer Yates out of commission, they are already low on personnel. If they have to protect you and search for whoever put the contract out on you, it will strain their manpower. So I propose we go into hiding for the time being. Let them search for the person behind the price on your head. I'll focus on keeping you and Ollie safe."

She nodded. It sounded like a good idea. So far.

"We're going to have to abandon your car at the first possible moment. It's too risky to hang on to it."

"Did you find us another car?" She hoped it wasn't stick shift. She never learned how to drive manual.

"I have one you might be able to use." Henry tossed her a key chain with a single key on it. "Unfortunately, it's not here. But it's close by. You can get it and leave your car in the pole barn. No one will go in there."

With every word, the situation felt more surreal.

Isaiah hefted a paper bag onto the table. "Henry also found us some different clothes to wear."

Tipping the bag over, he dumped its contents on the wooden surface. The first thing she saw was a small pair of dark trousers. Not denim, but not the same fabric she'd find at the local department store, either. That was followed by a blue long-sleeved shirt and blue suspenders. Isaiah handed her a wad of dark green. Warily, she accepted it, shaking it out, sending a small white bonnet flying. The long green dress was extreme in its simplicity. No lace or frills. No pockets. The cloth felt a bit scratchy. An over-dress of some kind in the same color came with it. She picked it up.

"That's the apron," Isaiah informed her.

Addie replaced the apron and stared at the clothes. She hazarded a guess.

"Are these Amish? We're dressing Amish?"

"It seems as good a disguise as any. The Amish keep to themselves, and while people are interested in them, I doubt too many would remember your face. They'd be more interested in what you wore."

She nodded. "I only see two sets of clothes here. For me and Ollie. What about you?"

Surely, he didn't plan on disguising them then dropping them off in Amish country to fend for themselves.

He hesitated. A tide of red swept up the back of his neck and the tips of his ears. "I have a set already. I lived here for a time when I was younger and left them behind when I left."

"So, you've pretended to be Amish before."

"Not exactly." His mouth twisted in a mocking grin. "I was Amish."

Whatever she'd expected him to say, it hadn't been that he used to be Amish. How did he go from that to becoming a bounty hunter?

EIGHT

"Thanks for everything, Henry." Isaiah stretched out his hand to his old friend.

"You know it." They shook once. "You'd best not stick around, Ice. Don't let them sneak up on you."

Ice? She bit back the question. She'd have plenty of time to ask in the car. Urgency flowed through her blood. What if someone reported seeing her car before they made it to the vehicle Henry was lending them? They'd be out of options. The adrenalin kicked in, and her heart raced so hard it felt like it would beat out of her chest. She placed a hand over her heart, pressing down as if she could slow its pace.

"Let's change and head out." Isaiah handed her the dress and the child's clothing. "You can use the bedroom on the left to change. There's not a lot of space in there, but you'll get the job done."

She took the clothes from him, flinching when his fingers brushed across the sensitive skin of her palm. It was fear. That was why her hands were trembling and her stomach fluttered.

Avoiding his gaze, she heralded Ollie into the room.

He hadn't lied. Once the door shut behind them, it was like trying to get ready in a tin can. If she had been claustrophobic, she'd be hyperventilating by now. Less than two feet existed between the door and the bunk beds with the handmade frame. If she turned to the left, she would run into open wooden storage lockers lining the wall, also handmade.

Quickly, she assisted Ollie in getting into the Amish outfit.

"Mommy, what about my shirt?" He held up the item in question. It was his favorite, with a large Tyrannosaurus rex on it.

"It'll be okay. We need to hide, so we have to dress different. Just for a little bit. Do you understand?"

He nodded. "We don't want the bad men to find us again."

Her heart ached that her innocent child seemed to feel this was a normal way to live, running from hired gunmen who wanted them dead. The memory of his shrieks while she was being strangled filled her ears for an instant.

A knock brought her back to her surroundings.

"Everything all right in there?" Isaiah's calm voice drifted through the heavy door.

"Yes. Ollie's ready. He's coming out so I can change."

Oliver grumbled but went with Isaiah when she shooed him from the bedroom. It only took her a few minutes to dress. The leggings and socks she pulled on were surprisingly warm. She'd wondered before how Amish women stayed warm in the winter wearing their simple dresses. Now she knew.

She had no idea what to do with the bonnet.

She left the room and went in search of Isaiah.

He narrowed his gaze when she returned to the main part of the cabin. She was being inspected. Finally, he nodded his approval.

"What do I do with this bonnet? And my hair?" She knew Amish women didn't wear their hair cascading down their backs.

"It's called a *kapp*, not a bonnet," he responded absently. "You have pretty hair."

She blinked at his announcement.

"You're right, though," he continued, as if

he hadn't said anything out of the ordinary. "Amish women don't wear their hair long. Only their husbands, and sometimes children, ever see their hair unbound. You'll braid it up or put it in a bun under the *kapp*."

"She probably shouldn't wear the *kapp* right away," Henry observed from his seat at the small table in the kitchen area. He bit into an apple. She could hear it crunching as he chewed from where she stood.

"Why not?" she asked him. If she was wearing the dress, wouldn't she need the hat, as well?

"Until you are out of the area, I think wearing an Amish *kapp* in a car will give you away. What Amish couple would be driving?"

Her heart fluttered at the concept of her and Isaiah being a couple. Foolishness.

"Hmmm." Isaiah rubbed his jaw. "You could be right. Although, they might assume we're Mennonite. Lots of *Englisch* don't know the difference."

"True. But why take the chance?"

"I have a scarf."

Both men turned her way. She fought not to squirm.

"A scarf?" Isaiah asked, flashing an encouraging smile.

"Yeah. You know, like a babushka. It's a scarf and hood combined. I can wear it over the *kapp* or leave the *kapp* off for now, and that way, anyone driving beside us will see me in a scarf. No one would think anything of it."

Henry frowned. "Your boy. He's diabetic?"

"Yes." She waited to see why he'd asked.

"Look, I don't know much about diabetes, but I know that diet is crucial. How are you on food?"

She hesitated. "We've gone through a bit of what I packed. His body doesn't produce the insulin needed to regulate his blood glucose levels. He needs a balance of protein and natural sugars, like fruits, to keep it level, plus insulin injections twice a day. I try to avoid too much processed stuff."

Now that they were on the run like this, she regretted not having him fitted with an insulin pump. His doctor had suggested it. She had wanted to wait until after the holidays so it wouldn't affect Ollie's enjoyment of Christmas.

"Look, I'm a bit of a health nut myself," Henry told her.

"That's putting it mildly," Isaiah muttered.

Henry ignored his friend. "Go ahead and raid my refrigerator. Take whatever you need for the kid."

Normally, she might have declined the offer out of pride. But this was her child's life. She'd always put her pride aside to ensure Ollie was well. He was her priority. "I appreciate it."

"Do you have any ice packs we can take, too?" Isaiah moved aside to allow her through as she headed to the kitchen. "I'll pay for them."

"Take 'em."

She raided the fridge and the cupboards, gathering an assortment of cheese, nuts, fruits, carrots and protein bars.

"Hard-boiled eggs in the door."

She paused in the middle of closing the appliance, reversing the action to snatch four of the eggs. Any more than that and she feared they might spoil. Isaiah grabbed the ice packs and threw them into the small ice chest they'd brought with them. Addie took down some bread and quickly made up some sandwiches for them. Then she cut up some of the cheese and lunch meat into cubes. Henry took a couple of plastic storage containers from the cupboard and handed them to her. She put the sandwiches in the larger container and the sliced up proteins in another.

"Ollie can have these for lunch. With an apple. And some water."

A diabetic would have to be careful of eating something with so many processed sugars, such as bread.

"I sure wish I had my duffel bag," Isaiah said suddenly. "I'm really glad I have my Taser and my Glock, but the rest of the stuff is gone. I don't want to borrow anything here that can be traced back to Henry."

She nodded, her stomach clenching. For someone to trace anything, they'd have to catch them. She didn't even want to contemplate what that would mean for them.

Glancing up, she caught the shadow of regret and sorrow flashing in Isaiah's bright blue eyes. Without thinking, she reached out and took his hand. "Thank you."

His face jerked to her, startled. "For helping you?"

She nodded. "Yes. But also for believing me. If you hadn't, we'd be dead."

He gave a one-shouldered shrug, clearly doubting her words.

"I'm serious, Isaiah. If you hadn't trusted your instincts about me, I, and possibly Ollie, would be dead right now."

Isaiah could do nothing to halt the shudder working its way down his spine at the vile idea of Addie and Ollie being dead. The calm manner in which she spoke magnified his horror. He turned away to hide his reaction, but the banana he'd eaten while waiting for her and Ollie to get dressed sat like lead in the pit of his stomach.

"We need to get a move on." Why was it so hard to discuss anything emotional? He'd always found it difficult.

Addie swept away to deal with her son. Shifting, his glance unconsciously sought hers. There was no irritation or impatience. Instead, her expression shone with compassion.

She didn't understand. If she knew.

He stopped that thought. No one—not even Henry and Zack—knew about the traumas that had formed Isaiah into the broken, closed-off person that he was. Those events had also sealed in him the need to seek out justice, even if that justice was come by in unusual ways.

After thanking Henry, he herded Addie and Ollie back out to the vehicle. They'd been at the hunting camp for almost two hours. Too long.

"Call me when you can, Ice. Let me know you made it."

"Will do." He gave a quick wave, then held the passenger door open for Addie. She had already fastened Ollie into his booster seat. One look at the boy's crossed arms and thrust-out bottom lip had Isaiah biting back a grin. Apparently, someone wasn't happy about returning to the car. He couldn't blame Ollie. He didn't want to drive again. His eyes were gritty from lack of sleep.

But he had to keep these two safe. It didn't matter how comfortable he was. They were what was important.

Buckling himself in, he started the vehicle and set it off down the long, rocky path that led to a two-lane highway. The gritters had been through earlier, the front plows on the large utility trucks clearing the snow away while the back dumped de-icer chemicals and coated the black tar surfaces with salt.

Isaiah waited for a car to pass before sliding out onto the road and heading away from Sutter Springs. He passed a road sign that said Thanks for Visiting Amish Country! It gave him a jolt. If he continued heading east, he'd practically drive right past his parents' property. He could see the place in his mind. Large white house with a wrap-around porch, grayish-blue door, the mare grazing in the fields and the building his *daed* did his carpentry work in.

Did Micah, Zeke or Gideon work for their father? Were they married?

A cold dread hit him. Were his parents still alive? Mentally, he pictured them as they were when he left, but fourteen years aged a person. They had to be nearing sixty, and though that wasn't old, the Amish way wasn't easy, and life wasn't always gentle.

He understood that as well as anyone.

"How did you find me?" Addie stretched out her legs in front of her. He didn't miss the way she winced. She'd been banged up in the past two days.

Isaiah shrugged. He didn't like talking about his life. Strangely, the moment he thought about it, the desire to share part of himself with her rose to the surface. He struggled with the impulse for a second before giving in. What harm could it be to tell her? He wouldn't tell her everything, but he could afford to answer a few questions without revealing himself to her.

It was a novelty, driving beside a fugitive that he actually liked and respected. Of course, he didn't believe she was the woman he'd been hired to find.

"It wasn't that hard." He looked in the rearview mirror. Still clear. "You changed your name, but you didn't change your whole identity. Once I knew your maiden name had been Bruce, I looked for both Addison Johnson and Addison Bruce. I didn't realize your son was a diabetic. Medical records are not something I can get into. However, talking to people who knew you, I found out he was sick, and knew you would need to live somewhere you'd have access to a pediatrician. I put out feelers and found you had been seen coming out of the Medical Center in Sutter Springs."

She looked shocked at how easily he'd found her. She cleared her throat.

"Is it dangerous? What you do?"

He nodded and pointed to the long scar on his cheek. "Sure is. I got this beauty when a fugitive pulled a hidden knife on me."

She sucked in a breath. "Oh, my. Did he get away?"

"Nah. I'm really good at wrestling and mixed martial arts. I got him restrained. He was a little bruised, but I didn't have to break anything. So that's a win." Suddenly, he needed her to know his one rule. "I have never killed anyone. Not while I was in the military, and not as a bounty hunter. I know I might have to one day, but I made a promise to myself that unless it was self-defense or someone else was in mortal peril, I would not kill."

"That seems odd, especially after seeing that arsenal you had with you."

"Ah! I miss my arsenal. I feel less prepared, not having all my tools available." He chuckled, although he was serious. Being unprepared left one vulnerable. "I don't always work alone. Sometimes Henry works with me. He's been planning on leaving the business, though."

"He seemed like a good friend."

"The best. We've been through a lot together. We served together for eight years."

"I didn't think the Amish entered the military."

"Ex-Amish." He bit off the words, then immediately regretted it when she flinched away. "Sorry. I don't talk about it."

She bit her lip. "Do you think the police really think I had something to do with Officer Yates getting shot?"

He went with the quick subject change and thought about his answer for a moment. "I hope not. Cops and I don't always see eye to eye. Some of them feel people like me get in their way. Yates didn't feel that way, but I could tell Lieutenant Bartlett wasn't easily convinced of your innocence."

"I thought she was nice."

He grinned. "Nice, huh? She reminded me

of a stalking tiger. Very patient and observing. I looked into her record while you were sleeping at the hotel. She's solid. Her record is spotless. She's been decorated several times. I think she'll be a strong ally, once she knows the truth."

Beside him, Addie let out a bark of sarcastic laughter. "The truth? How can we tell her that when we don't know the full truth?"

He lifted his hand from the steering wheel and reached out, covering her hands, clasped in her lap. She froze. He removed his hand, shocked at his instinctual move to provide comfort. He didn't touch people. Not ever.

"Sorry. I know we don't know the truth yet. But we will. I need to get you to safety. We need to clear your name so other bounty hunters don't come after you. My contract ends in nine days."

"Nine days!" she exclaimed. "What does that mean?"

"It means that if I don't bring you in by that date, I will no longer be under contract, and they will hire someone else to find you and bring you in."

She slumped into her seat, her eyes dazed. "This is unreal. What a way to spend Christmas."

"Mommy. I'm hungry."

They both groaned at the interruption. Then he threw her a grin. She smiled back. It was genuine, although tension remained carved into the otherwise smooth skin around her lips.

"I should have expected this." She glanced at the clock. "He had his snack almost three hours ago. It's well past lunch time."

She reached back and grabbed at the bags of food on the floorboard behind the driver's seat. She then twisted the cap off a water bottle and handed it to Isaiah. "I'm glad you put the cooler so close."

He accepted the drink gratefully and took a swallow. Placing it in the cupholder next to hers, he waited until she handed Ollie his lunch. "Small bites," she reminded her son. "And chew it well."

"I know that, Mommy." The irritation in the little voice was precious.

She rolled her eyes. "I forget that he knows everything."

Isaiah couldn't hold in his snicker. "He's got nothing on my brother, Gideon. He was the smartest kid I ever knew. Probably gifted by today's standards. When he was a kid, he was so obnoxious with his know-it-all attitude. It was a good thing he was cute."

He realized what he'd said and slammed his

lips shut. He never talked about his family. To anyone. Yet with her, he'd talked about Gideon as if she had the right to know. As if it was something he did daily.

She raised her eyebrows, curiosity radiating from her, but didn't ask. He had a feeling she'd wait until little ears weren't listening. He appreciated her sensitivity.

When she handed him the sandwiches, he nodded his thanks.

The smell of eggs filled the car as she took one of the hard-boiled eggs for herself. She offered him one. He made a gagging sound and shook his head.

"Yeah, no. I can't eat 'em that way."

They settled into a comfortable silence, punctuated by crunching and slurping from Ollie as he ate and drank his water. A small dribble ran down his chin, but otherwise, the kid managed fine. Addie laughed, handed him a napkin, then gathered the remainder of their lunch together and placed all the trash in a grocery-store bag and tied it up. It all seemed so normal, almost like having a family.

No. He couldn't think that way. Soon, he would be separating from them, and hopefully, they'd be out of danger by then.

He couldn't forget there was a ticking clock.

A deer ran across the road in front of him. Tightening his hands on the wheel, Isaiah depressed the brake pedal. Nothing. He pushed harder. His front bumper missed the leaping animal by two inches.

"Isaiah!" Addie shouted, bracing her arm against the dashboard.

The brake pedal was on the floor of the car. The road crested and began a sharp downward slope.

"We have no brakes!" Isaiah ground out. "I can't stop."

The vehicle hurtled down the incline, moving faster every second. If they hit ice, or if they came to a traffic light with other vehicles, someone would die.

NINE

Her heart solidly in her throat, Addie glued her eyes to the rising needle on the speedometer. Fifty. Fifty-five. Sixty. Sixty-five. Seventy.

Tearing her gaze away, she began praying. The speed limit was forty-five. Except for when they'd been chased, he'd been driving as close to the limit as possible since they picked up her car earlier. No doubt because they couldn't afford to get stopped for speeding or erratic driving.

"Isaiah." Was that her voice? She barely recognized the taut tone, dragging out his name like a piece of soft taffy.

"I'm thinking," he said, tightly controlled, but she saw his hands, white knuckled on the steering wheel.

"Could your mechanic have done something to the brakes?"

"No. Kevin is a friend. If one of his cars broke or crashed, he'd take it as a personal hit on his reputation."

She stopped speaking as a cat ran across the road. She squeezed her lids shut.

The vehicle swerved. Her stomach followed.

"We missed it."

Her eyes flew open.

"How far until we hit a light? Or enter a town?"

The steep incline began to level out. She let out a breath as the speedometer crept back down to sixty. It wasn't forty-five, but it was better than seventy.

"Ten miles."

"Should we turn onto a dirt road?" They had just whizzed past two such roads. Surely the dirt and gravel would slow their trajectory.

"Better not." They were coming up to two cars. One was already in the passing lane, going way too slow. Both lanes were good and blocked. They were going to hit one of the cars. Isaiah veered onto the shoulder and whipped past the two vehicles, clipping the driver's mirror on the other car. The horn blared.

"Sorry," he muttered.

There was no way to stop.

"See that? I was able to use the shoulder

to miss the cars. Dirt roads have no wiggle room. And kids tend to run out on them without thinking because the traffic is slower. Not to mention the trouble we'll be in if we hit the mud and slush and skid."

Horror at the picture he painted filled her mind.

They had no option. They had to keep going. Unless they could somehow slow down.

"Isaiah, if you continued to drive along the shoulder, could you slow it down?"

He briefly looked her way. "Maybe so."

She could hear it now, the flavor of the Amish language in his tone. In the lilt of the words, the slightly fuller sound of the vowels. She hadn't noticed it earlier.

He pulled over to the shoulder. The car vibrated and a loud rumbling noise grated through the air. The tires would be shredded if they drove like this for a long time, but it was serving its purpose. Little by little, Addie's car was losing momentum.

The car they'd clipped pulled up beside them. Honking. He looked really mad. His window rolled down, and he yelled at them. She rolled down her window, keeping her scarf tight around her head.

"Pull over! I need to make an accident report!" The wind carried most of the sound away. She knew he was shouting, but only a fragment of the volume drifted through the window.

"Can't!" she yelled back. "No brakes!"

The moment he smiled, she knew she'd made a mistake. A dreadful one. He pulled out a gun and aimed it at her. She saw her name on his lips.

He was out to collect fifty thousand dollars over her dead body.

"Isaiah!"

Isaiah jerked the wheel, yanking them back onto the road. The front end smashed into the hired killer's wheel well. Both vehicles shuddered.

Isaiah hit the gas pedal. They had no brakes but couldn't afford to slow down until they were out of range of the man's gun.

Addie's car ripped past him. The killer tried to follow. His engine revved.

Glancing back, she saw him picking up speed. It wouldn't be long until they were neck and neck again. And what happened now? The next town continued to loom ahead of them. They wouldn't be able to continue as they were for more than a few minutes. Then they'd have to take their chances on a dirt road or find a new plan.

The closer they drove to the next town, the more traffic merged onto the two-lane highway. Isaiah zoomed into the left lane to avoid a pickup truck. Their tail copied his move. Zipping back to the right lane, he slid between two tractor trailers. Unfortunately, he was moving too fast to remain there.

He swerved back into the left lane as the killer gained on them. Glancing back, Addie saw a rifle emerge from the passenger-side window.

"A gun!" she yelled. "He has a rifle."

"Get down!"

Addie glanced into the back seat. Ollie's head rose an inch above the back of the leather bench thanks to his booster chair. She unbuckled her seatbelt, ignoring Isaiah's order to stay where she was. Climbing over the arm rest in the middle, she stumbled into the back seat, landing next to her son. She pulled his seatbelt loose.

"Mommy! We're not s'posed to!" Ollie exclaimed, his big eyes terrified.

"I know, little man. This is an emergency. We have to sit on the floor."

She tugged him from the seat and they crouched on the back floorboard together. Just in time. The back window smashed, raining glass over the booster seat and the leather seat.

Oliver screamed. She held him close. His scream cut off, replaced by scared sobs. Her heart broke. No child should ever have to live in fear.

"Hold on!" Isaiah called grimly. "We have to get enough distance between us before I can attempt to stop this beast again."

If they hadn't been running for their lives, she might have protested the derogatory name for her old beater. Right now, all she could think of was that someone would die before this was over. She'd gladly give her life if it meant Ollie was safe.

And Isaiah.

She didn't know him well. But he had proven himself a good man willing to do what was right, regardless of the personal cost. She hoped helping her didn't cost him his life.

A strange ding chimed.

"What was that?" she frowned.

"Um, Addie. Your low-fuel light came on."

She squeezed her eyes closed and wrapped her arms around her son. How could this day get any worse? No brakes. A killer on their tail. Innocent people ahead of them. And they were going to soon run out of gas and become little more than sitting ducks.

"Hold tight. There's an exit to the interstate in half a mile. We can take that, and maybe buy ourselves a little more space."

She didn't reply. She was nearly out of hope. Laying her cheek against Ollie's hair, she prayed.

"Help us, Lord."

Isaiah heard her praying over the roar of the engine. The hopelessness in her words hit him like a punch in the gut. He'd brought her out here. He would get her and Ollie to safety.

The ramp for the interstate was drawing closer. Glancing in the rearview, the other car remained behind them. The front driver-side wheel seemed to be wobbling. His muscles tightened as the exit came in range. When he pressed the gas, the car shot forward, surging onto the ramp. Inertia kept the vehicle flying forward. He gripped the wheel, forcing it to follow the curve.

Another glance back. The killer hadn't been deterred. His vehicle swerved on the winding ramp and kept pace.

Isaiah merged onto the interstate. The traffic was flowing more, which was good and bad. It was good because it hid them more. But he worried that the killer would pull out the gun again and shoot, possibly hitting an innocent bystander in the process.

He glanced back in time to see the hitman's front wheel wobble and collapse, disabling the car.

"Addie, look!"

She shoved herself up from the floorboard and checked the view behind them. A disbelieving laugh fell from her lips. "Did his wheel fall off?"

Isaiah laughed, too, relief flooding him. He relaxed his grip on the steering wheel, flexing his fingers to work out the ache from clenching them so tight. "It did. I must have hit it just right."

"That was God at work. He knew we would need to escape."

Isaiah wasn't sure how to respond to that. He and God hadn't been close for years. God certainly hadn't rescued Raymond. Or Christina. The list of people that Isaiah had seen suffering and in pain during his life would fill several notebooks. So many innocents who had their lives disrupted and destroyed by the wickedness pervading the world.

And God let it happen.

Isaiah pushed aside the guilt such thoughts provoked. His *mamm* would be so disappointed in him if she could see him. See how little faith he had left. That was one more thing that had kept him from reaching out to his family for all the long years apart.

He was no longer the son and brother they had known. He wouldn't fit into their family. Not anymore.

"Can you put Ollie back in his booster seat?" he asked, changing the subject.

"It's covered with glass. Everything is."

That was a problem.

They also needed gas, but literally couldn't stop the car. And they were on an interstate with a child out of his booster chair. It was enough to make him wish he was a praying man. Almost.

A final glance back in his rearview mirror showed their pursuer was nowhere in sight. Hopefully, the car's wheel falling off would keep the hitman out of commission long enough for Isaiah to get Addie and Ollie to safety.

A mile down the road, his hopes, which had begun to hesitantly rise again, sank. The car began to shiver and shake, and the engine made an awful rubbing sound.

"What's happening?" Addie's voice drifted up from behind his seat.

The car spluttered and gasped. He eased it over to the embankment. It died. He hit the hazard lights, which began to blink, warning oncoming cars. The traffic continued to move past. Thankfully, most of the vehicles moved over to the left lane when they saw the car dead on the shoulder.

"We were low on gas. We'll have to travel on foot."

There was a moment of silence. Then she said, "I thought when the low-fuel light went on you had twenty-five miles until the tank was empty. There is no way we drove half that distance."

"True. I would say, on top of everything else, you have a faulty gas gauge."

The sound she made could only be described as a low growl.

He unhooked his buckle and pushed his door open in order to exit the car. "Stay where you are. I will come around the passenger side for you."

Climbing out, he scanned the area, searching for any signs of impending danger. Not finding any, he jogged around to the back passenger door and helped them out. "Take only what is critical. We have to abandon everything else."

At his words, Ollie tightened his small arms around the stuffed dog he carried everywhere. His face tilted up to Isaiah, silently pleading with him. Isaiah knew that if he started to shake his head no, that pleading expression would disappear and in a flash he'd be facing serious defiance. It wasn't a battle worth fighting at the moment. Things were hard enough for the child. He wasn't about to strip him of the one object that comforted him.

"Take good care of Bowie." He ruffled his hair. "He's going to depend on you."

"I will," Ollie promised solemnly.

Addie stepped out of the vehicle. Turning, she tugged out a backpack and proceeded to dump out all the Englisch clothes she'd brought. Then she shoved the small ice pack with Ollie's supplies and whatever food would fit inside it.

He admired her more at that moment than he could say. He saw the clothes she left behind.

Although not fancy, they were good clothes, made from good cloth. Definitely not cheap. But she willingly abandoned them without a complaint.

She caught him looking at her. "We're going to have to be Amish for a bit. It was a good thing I hadn't been wearing the *kapp* earlier. That would have made this disguise useless."

She tied on the *kapp* and gave him a thumbs up. They were ready to move.

"We don't want to backtrack. They might be heading this way. But if we keep along the road, we risk the possibility of them catching up to us and recognizing us, even dressed this way. After all, once they see that we're not with your car, they'll know we went somewhere else."

It was a quandary.

A truck pulled up next to them. The man rolled down the passenger window. "Need some help, folks?"

Isaiah looked at the man. It was like looking into the past. "Jerry Karns."

He and Raymond used to help Jerry pick rocks out of the fields of his father's dairy farm. The cows would injure themselves if it wasn't done on a regular basis.

The man startled. His eyebrows hid beneath his hair. "No. It can't be. Isaiah?"

Isaiah nodded.

"What—" Jerry started to ask.

Isaiah cut him off. "I'm in trouble, Jerry. I can't talk out in the open."

Immediately, the man's friendly expression became concerned. He leaned across the seat and pushed the door open.

"Hop in. I'll give you a ride."

Isaiah didn't have the luxury of time to decide if this was a good idea or not. He had to protect two people. He assisted them into the back seat of the extended cab, then sat next to Jerry on the front seat.

"Lorraine's not going to believe this," Jerry chuckled with relish. "I can never surprise that woman. But this will."

Isaiah smiled. Jerry was a couple of years older than him. He and Lorraine had been a couple since they met. "You married her, yes?"

"I married her the moment we graduated from college. And you remember Scott?"

Isaiah grinned. Scott was Jerry's younger brother. "Sure do."

"He married his high-school sweetheart,

Mary Beth, six months before I got hitched. They've got three girls."

"Unreal." He shook his head, a pang of remorse echoing in his soul. He'd missed so much.

"I just saw your brother Zeke the other day," Jerry said. "He said nothing about you being back."

This was going to be awkward. "Umm. I'm not. I haven't seen my family since I left."

Jerry's head wagged, his disapproval evident. "Not cool, Isaiah. Your parents are good people. They've been through a lot."

He winced at the reminder. "I know. Listen, I'm in the area accidentally. This wasn't planned."

Ollie leaned forward, his dog shoved under his chin. "Mean people were shooting at Mommy and me." He piped up before anyone could shush him. "Mr. Isaiah is helping us."

If Jerry's eyes grew any wider, they'd pop clear out of his skull. "What does he mean—"

"Look, Jerry. I can't answer all your questions. I will answer what I can. But first, I need to get Addie and Ollie someplace safe. Ollie was telling the truth. There are people chasing us."

Jerry set his jaw and pressed the gas pedal harder. The truck rumbled and picked up speed until the needle hovered around the sixty-eight miles per hour mark. Then he punched the button on his dashboard for his phone.

"Jerry? Is everything all right?" a woman's voice answered.

"Everything's fine, Lorraine. I ran into a friend. Isaiah. He and his…family need a place to stay overnight. Do you think we have room?"

"We do. But remember, I'm off to my mother's this evening. I won't be home until tomorrow."

Isaiah sagged in his seat. They wouldn't have to make excuses to Jerry's wife. He had always liked Lorraine, and despite his job, he couldn't stand deceit of any kind. If he could tell the truth, he would.

"Oh, that's right. I forgot about that, dear."

"Should I cancel?" Lorraine worried. "I wouldn't want to offend your friends."

"No, that's all right. I'll tell you everything when I see you in the morning. I'm actually glad you won't be there. He's in a spot of trouble, and I think he'll be more comfortable talking to me alone."

"We'll if you're sure…"

"Love you, dear."

Jerry hung up. "I won't tell her anything you say I can't. But she deserves to know what happens in her house and who stays there."

Isaiah was concerned that Jerry had given Lorraine his first name, but let it go. There was nothing to be done about it. And she hadn't seemed to connect the name with him, so chances were there was nothing to worry about.

The way to Jerry's house was silent. When they arrived, they were just in time to see Jerry's wife off. She greeted Isaiah with a smile on her face. The smile faded when she looked at him straight on. He groaned when the recognition dawned.

"As I live and breathe. Isaiah Bender." She clasped her hands together at her breast. "We have prayed for your return for years. Oh, how wonderful for your family! First your sister is found, and now the prodigal son returns!"

He staggered back a foot. "Christina—my sister was found?"

She stilled, her hand flying to her mouth. "You don't know."

He stared at her, unable to respond. His brain seemed to be frozen. Finally, he managed to shake his head.

Lorraine smiled, teary-eyed. "Yes, she was found about four or five years ago. She's married now, to a police officer, I believe."

Isaiah swallowed. "Lorraine, I appreciate you letting us stay for the night. My friend is in trouble, and Jerry agreed to help me."

"Will you tell me later what's going on?"

He nodded. "When I can."

If he could. He couldn't promise they'd still be there in the morning. The last thing he'd do is repay their kindness by sticking around and bringing danger to their doorstep.

TEN

Christina had returned. Isaiah couldn't wrap his mind around it. His baby sister, lost since she was two, had come back. He waited until Lorraine had left, then ambushed Jerry the moment he stepped through the door.

"How? How did my sister come back?"

Jerry held up his hands as if warding off an attack. "I'll tell you what I know. But let's go to the kitchen first. I need to eat."

That reminded him of Ollie. Isaiah looked at Addie. She nodded.

"Okay. Our little boy here might need something, too. He's diabetic."

Addie tilted her head. He thought back to what he said and flushed. He had made it sound like Ollie was his. "I mean, well, he's not my son. But he does need his levels checked."

Jerry chuckled at his show of embarrassment. He remembered that about Jerry. He found amusement in the strangest things. The group moved to the other room. Jerry put a kettle of water on the stove. "Anyone want tea? I don't drink coffee anymore, but my wife keeps Pepsi in the fridge. Or there's water."

"Water's fine for me." Isaiah grimaced. He'd never developed a taste for tea or soda. He was strictly a water or black coffee kind of guy.

"Tea would be lovely," Addie said. She looked at Ollie's numbers and frowned. "Ollie could use some water."

Concerned, Isaiah stepped to her side. He kept his tone light, so he didn't alarm Ollie. "Is there a problem?"

Jerry twisted to face them at the sink.

Addie glanced between the two men. "Not really. His glucose is a little lower than normal. It hasn't been that long since lunch. I think he's a little dehydrated. That can affect his numbers."

She might be smiling, but Isaiah detected the fear she was attempting to hide. He put a hand on her shoulder, lending her his support. She sent him a grateful smile.

Jerry sauntered to the fridge. "Of course he can have some water. Your son is welcome to whatever he needs."

A spattering of scratches came from the corner, followed by the distinct clicking of claws on the kitchen flooring. A small dog peeked out at them. He was white, with light brown splotches covering his body and circling one eye. His cockeyed ears perked up, and he padded over to Ollie, laid his head on the boy's knee and then gave him the most pathetic whine Isaiah had ever heard.

Isaiah rubbed his hand over his mouth to disguise the smile he couldn't stop from spreading across his face. He slid a glance to Addie, expecting her to be smiling. She wasn't. She eyed the dog with suspicion.

"Don't worry about the dog, ma'am. He's a baby, really. Very gentle. We have chickens, and he won't even chase after them. Now my other dog, she'll chase after anything. This guy, he only wants to sleep and cuddle."

Ollie slid off his chair the moment his water was gone and put his nose against the dog's. When the dog reacted with a wet, slobbery kiss on his nose, Ollie giggled and wrapped his arms around his neck. Addie leaned forward, alarmed.

"Buster won't hurt him, ma'am."

She subsided, but remained tense, waiting.

"Maybe this conversation can wait until he goes to sleep this evening," Isaiah murmured. He didn't want to wait, but he also didn't want to have the conversation in front of Oliver.

It was a long evening. Isaiah considered himself to be a patient man, but his nerves were stretched so tight, he imagined he could hear them squeak when he moved. Addie settled down on the couch beside him. Ollie was looking at books on his mother's phone, and Buster was tucked up against his side. Jerry had gone to finish his evening chores in his barn. Isaiah had offered to assist. It might have been many years since he'd milked a cow, but he still understood the process.

"Nah. You stay here. I expect you need to keep a low profile."

Which meant he was inside, waiting, when he would have preferred to be busy.

"How do you think we'll ever separate them, now?" Addie pointed at the pair on the floor. They had fallen asleep.

Isaiah shook his head. "It won't be easy."

"Hey, I don't know what happened with your sister. Or what you're going through now. If you need me to listen, I will."

He reached out and took her hand, squeezing it once before releasing it to let it lie on the couch between them. Unwilling to completely break the connection, he left his hand lying next to hers, barely touching.

"I appreciate it. I don't normally talk about it, but this time, I will take you up on the offer. Right now, it's a lot to process." He paused, thinking. "My sister was kidnapped when she was two. I was only four. My memories are vague, but I do remember that it changed how my whole family functioned. For years, *Mamm* would cry at unexpected moments. When my cousin got married and had a baby, she asked *Mamm* if she could name her baby Christina. *Mamm* said of course, but later that night, I heard her sobbing. When people hear that someone had a child abducted, sometimes they think that the pain fades after a few years. But it doesn't."

"How can it?" she murmured. "There is no closure. No understanding of where your child is. And the fear that your child might be suffering or in pain. It has to be agonizing."

He sighed. "You get it."

"I've never experienced it. It's every mother's worst nightmare. Last summer, I took Ollie to the zoo. He was supposed to hold my hand at all times. But he got excited at the penguin exhibit and ran toward it. I lost him in the crowd. For two minutes, I couldn't find him. I thought my heart would stop. I found him. A young woman was trying to coax him to go with her."

He shot a glance at her face. She almost lost her son.

She nodded. "It was too close. I've never forgotten the feeling. It was bad for a few minutes. Your parents must have felt that way for years."

"They did," Jerry said, entering behind them. He put more wood on the fire. Isaiah picked up Ollie and carried him into the room that Addie and Ollie would share that night. Addie, who had followed, pulled down the covers and took off Ollie's shoes. Isaiah and Addie tiptoed back to the living room. The fire was roaring in the fireplace, filling the room with a warm glow. Jerry plugged in the Christmas tree. The lights blinked. A few gifts were under the tree.

It was an enchanting picture.

One he had no hope of for himself.

Isaiah settled back on the couch. "Jerry, tell me about Christina."

"First, it's Joss now."

"Joss?"

"She wasn't raised Amish. Anyway, your brother Micah found her."

He blinked. "Micah?"

"Yep."

Isaiah thought for a moment. "Micah left the Amish before I did. Did he keep his connection with the family?"

"It was strained for a few years, but yeah, he did. He is a deputy US marshal now."

"He's a what?"

"You heard me. He found her. She's back and, like Lorraine said, is married to a Sutter Springs Police Officer. They have a couple of kids."

"What about Zeke and Gideon?"

"Well, Gideon's still single. Zeke, though, he married a woman a few years back. She died and he recently remarried. A sweet young thing. Molly Schultz."

"Molly! I remember her family. Wow. Things have changed." He shook his head. Would he even recognize his own family if he saw them again? Suddenly, the longing in his chest made it difficult to breathe. They were so close. *Mamm*, *Daed*, Zeke and Gideon were still in the Amish community. And even Micah and Christina—Joss—were part of the family.

The only one missing was him.

"What I want to know about," Jerry stood to put another log on the fire, "is what happened to you."

He couldn't tell Jerry about Raymond. Not yet. At least not the part Jerry didn't know.

"I left after Raymond was killed."

"I remember that. What I want to know is why."

He stood and began pacing the room. "I can't tell you that. What I can tell you is that after I left, I earned my GED and then I spent eight years in the Marines. Straight infantry. When I returned, I didn't have many options. I didn't want to go into the police. The Marines would have paid for college, but it wasn't a good fit for me. But the Marines had given me training and skills. So, I became a bounty hunter."

"No way!" Jerry's eyes bulged out. "What does a bounty hunter do?"

"When people don't show up for court or violate their probation, a warrant is put out on them. Bounty hunters are hired to bring them in. I get paid when I bring in a fugitive."

"Not as glamourous as I thought." Jerry pulled a face. "How does Addie fit into it?"

"She's a woman who is being stalked. I agreed to help her."

It was too dangerous to reveal the real story. He might trust Jerry, but the fewer people aware of who she really was, the safer she'd be.

He hoped.

Later that night, he stretched out on the couch, trying to sleep. His mind refused to cooperate. The evening's conversations swirled through his mind. He didn't know how. He didn't even know if they'd accept him back, after the life he'd lived, but it was time to try and patch things up with his family. He didn't know if their relationship could be mended, but he'd regret it forever if he didn't try. If they couldn't accept him, he'd at least have seen them one more time.

Finally, he fell into a fitful sleep. When a cold draft awakened him, he opened one eye to find it was barely past five in the morning and Jerry was moving around to do morning chores. Groaning, Isaiah flopped over on his other side, determined to sleep for one more hour, at least.

It was futile. Between the noise Jerry made clumping around in the kitchen and the faint light beginning to filter through the blinds, he knew he'd get no more sleep this morning. Grumbling under his breath, he flung off the blankets his old friend had found for him and made his way into the kitchen.

"I found this in the cupboard." Jerry slid a glass jar of instant coffee his way. Not his favorite, but he needed caffeine. And it was still better than tea.

"Thanks, man. I need this."

"Not a problem. I need to run into town after chores to get a few things. I'll leave you guys on your own for a bit. That okay?"

"Yep. I appreciate all you've done for us."

"Like I said, it's all good. Friends do that."

It was just after eight when Jerry pulled out of the driveway.

"Are you okay?" Addie appeared at his shoulder. "That discussion was intense last night."

He glanced over at her. Standing in the light streaming through the window, she seemed to glow. If they were married, he'd have the right to kiss her good morning. She had a very kissable mouth.

Whoa. That thought did not go through his head. He couldn't think of her that way. Even if she was an amazing woman and mother, and even if she did smell like coconut, he could not risk losing his head over her. He had enough troubles. Not to mention her current situation. No. He needed to keep himself under control.

Even as he cautioned himself, he knew it wasn't his head that was in trouble. It was his heart.

She'd seen the glance he'd tossed her way. For a single breathless moment, she was sure Isaiah Bender intended to kiss her. What really shocked her was she knew she'd let him.

Then he'd backed off, physically and emotionally, and she knew the moment was gone. She sighed. He was the first man to touch her heart since her husband died.

"Jerry's out. He'll be back later."

She nodded, unsure what to say next. An awkward silence fell. Was he contemplating the kiss that wasn't, like she was? She puttered around, trying to keep busy to keep her mind off him. Several times, she realized she'd been staring at him too long. Would she ever stop blushing? Honestly, she was acting like a lovesick teenager. She hadn't been that bad when she was a teen.

"What happened to your friend Raymond?"

Did that question really fly out of her mouth? She hadn't intended on asking him, although she'd been curious since she heard the incident referred to the night before. For a moment, she thought he'd ignore her question. She wouldn't blame him if he did. It was none of her business how his childhood friend had died.

"It's not a pretty story," he shocked her by saying.

"If you don't want to tell—"

"I have never talked about it." He turned to face her and leaned back against the counter. "Raymond and I were best friends. We did everything together. We even picked rocks with Jerry and his brother Scott during the summer."

She sipped at her tea, making no comments lest he change his mind about telling her the story.

"When we were sixteen, we went hunting together. Raymond was pumped. He'd bought a new gun and had never used it before. When he saw a deer, he took aim, and the gun misfired. He died in my arms."

Her hand covered her mouth. It was so much worse than she'd expected.

"The final straw was that the man who sold

him the gun knew it wasn't functioning right. Knew, in fact, that the gun was stolen. He was so concerned with making a profit, he sold a broken, illegal gun, and my best friend lost his life."

He pushed away from the counter and stalked around the edges of the small room. "When his parents were made aware of it, they were devastated. And the man who had sold the gun got off on a technicality."

"Isaiah." She had no idea what to say.

He halted and pivoted to face her. "At that moment, I lost some of my faith. Or at least, I thought I did. I've been thinking about God more lately."

"That's why you became a bounty hunter. Because of Raymond." It made sense, in a sad way. He must have felt so angry. Angry, scared and helpless. She didn't comment on his loss of faith. He was finding his way back; that was the important thing. And, she had to admit, sometimes faith became stronger when it was questioned. If you believed simply because your parents did or you were supposed to, it was never really your faith.

He nodded. "Yeah. And also because of my sister. I didn't remember her very well, but I knew the affects her loss had on my family. It became an obsession for me."

His story broke her heart. She set her tea aside and walked over to him. Without a word, she wrapped her arms around his waist and hugged him, her head on his chest. The steady pounding of his heart echoed in her ear. It was an embrace meant to comfort, to wordlessly tell him she understood and cared. He tensed in her arms. She loosened her grip and prepared to drop her arms and step away to give him space. That idea altered when his arms came up and slid around her. His chin rested on her hair.

For the moment, they were in perfect harmony.

Until…

"Why are you hugging Mr. Isaiah, Mommy?"

The adults broke apart, laughing. She caught his eye briefly, her face flushed. He didn't look embarrassed. Rather, his expression was… peaceful. In a way she had never seen before.

"I'm hugging Mr. Isaiah because he was a little sad," she explained to Ollie. Immediately, the little boy flew to Isaiah and threw his arms around his waist.

"Mommy hugs me when I'm sad, too. It makes me feel better."

Isaiah swallowed. Ollie released him and ran over to Buster.

Isaiah leaned down and pressed a kiss on her forehead.

"What was that for?"

"Thank you. I didn't know how much I needed to talk. I feel better. Like I'm lighter."

She nodded her understanding. Trauma could spill its own special brand of poison into your heart and soul if you didn't work to eradicate it. He'd allowed it to fester.

"I'm going to make sure the fire's going. Don't want Jerry coming home to a cold house, *ja*?"

She blinked at him. He hadn't been Amish for fourteen years. In the past day, she had heard a couple of phrases, caught a cadence in his speech, that remained from that time. Such as now. Seeing him in his Amish clothes, she could imagine him living that life.

She would never have met him had he stayed. A shiver racked her body. Another bounty hunter may not have seen, or cared about, the signs that she wasn't the fugitive they sought. Would she have been dead if someone else had found her?

God's providence amazed her. No matter

how complicated her world was, how bad life seemed, He showed her again and again that He was bigger and stronger than any problems the world could dish out.

He was her peace in the storm.

She needed to keep her hands and mind busy. Jerry had said to help themselves, so she took him at his word and fixed a quick breakfast. When Isaiah wandered back in fifteen minutes later, she pointed to the table and the three of them ate.

"What's the plan?" She carried her empty plate to the sink. "Ollie, you can play in the living room. Stay away from doors and windows, and if you see anyone other than Mr. Isaiah, Mr. Jerry or myself, you come immediately to us."

He nodded and ran from the room, Buster on his tail.

"The dog will warn us if anyone comes around."

"That's one plus to having a dog around."

"Yeah. Anyway, about the plan. I don't know that I have one. We can't stay here. I would like to keep moving east. I also looped Henry in this morning and asked if he could do some of the legwork. I tried calling Chad Whitman, the man who contracted me to find you and bring you in."

She whirled around to face him, the blood leaving her face so fast, white noise filled her ears.

He leaped toward her, nudging her into a chair before the sudden dizziness made her fall.

"Not to turn you in. You know that!" His voice had an accusing edge.

"I know that," she murmured. She searched his face. "It shocked me, that's all, hearing that you tried to call him."

He pushed a strand of hair behind her ear. The warmth of his touch lingered. "I wanted to see if I could stall. But it doesn't matter. The number he gave me was no longer in service."

She scrunched her forehead, confused. "Why wouldn't he try and call you to give you an updated number?"

"If he's involved with the people coming after you, he wouldn't want to be traced."

She sucked in a breath. "And that means the person who put a price on my head knows you're with me."

"Exactly. Which means he's after us both. I sent Henry a text and told him to go off-grid.

He's a known associate of mine. He knows how to hide, so I'm not concerned. He's checking the identity of the bondsman who hired me. Digging up intel about whether he's legit. My gut tells me it was all a setup to get to you. The contract, the look-alike and the reward. It's all connected."

Her heart lodged firmly in her throat, she stared at him. What had she ever done to incur such wrath? With so many people coming after them, would any of them make it out of this alive?

ELEVEN

She looked stunned. Isaiah had an inkling of what was going through Addie's mind. Probably the same thing that was buzzing around in his. The whole situation was spinning wildly out of control.

It bothered Isaiah, thinking that he had been used to trap her. His question was why? There were so many whys. Why was someone after Addie? Why did they pick him to chase her down? Was he picked deliberately, or was it a random choice? And why was a man with a stellar reputation like Chad Whitman hiring a bounty hunter to track down an innocent woman?

Another thought snuck into his head. Maybe Chad wasn't the person who had contacted him. After all, a decoy had been used to frame Addie. Which brought up another point. Why go through the charade of having her arrested if you were going to send hired killers after her?

Too many moving parts.

And now he had gotten Henry and his old friend Jerry involved right smack in the middle of it all. For that, his regret ran deep. He could only pray that they would be safe.

The moment the thought entered his consciousness, he halted where he stood. The idea of praying for something had not come naturally to him for fourteen years or more. Yet, he could not shake the sense it was time.

He didn't even know how to begin to formulate a prayer for all the things on his mind.

And he couldn't start praying in front of Addison. That would be too awkward. Not that she would judge him. He had learned enough about Addie to know that judgment was not part of her makeup. No, he was just feeling insecure and needed to be alone in order to make those first steps.

"I'm going to take a look around outside. Check the place out and see if anything is going on."

When she agreed, he pushed open the back door and walked out. First, he made good on his promise and checked out the property.

When he didn't see anything out of place and nothing raised any red flags in his mind, he began to pray.

"God," he began, his breath puffing out in clouds with each breath, "I need a favor."

He winced. That sounded juvenile. Like he was bartering with God. However, he knew that God would understand his heart. Shaking his head, he decided to stop worrying about if his words were right and just say what was on his mind.

Pouring out his heart and soul had never come easy to him. But with each word it got easier. Ten minutes later, he walked back into the house. The phone was ringing. Since it wasn't his house or his phone, he didn't answer it.

The answering machine kicked on. Lorraine's sweet voice rang out, asking the caller to leave a message. When it beeped, he was already walking out of the room.

"Isaiah!" Jerry's urgent voice whisper-yelled down the line. "Pick up the phone. Right. Now."

He was picking it up before the last word was done.

"Jerry?"

"Put the call on speaker. We don't have time for you to repeat this."

Isaiah turned to motion Addie closer, only to

find she was at his side, wringing a dish cloth in her grasp. He held the receiver away from his face and pushed the speaker button.

"Done."

"Good. Now listen here. Lorraine called. She and her mother were out this morning. They went into a shop. A man was there, and he had pictures. One was of Addie. The other one was you, Isaiah. He was looking for you. My Lorraine is smart and didn't say anything. But one of the other patrons saw the picture of you and said they'd seen you in my truck yesterday. Lorraine denied it. She said you haven't been in contact with your family in nearly fifteen years, as far as she knew. They're coming for you, Isaiah. Get your girl and her kid, and get out of there."

Isaiah had lead in his belly. "Don't come home, Jerry. These guys, they are killers. And tell Lorraine she and her mother need to go somewhere. Don't worry about packing. Just go."

"I already told her that. They left straight from the store and are heading away from her mother's house."

"Thanks for the heads up."

"Do me one more favor? Take Buster."

"Will do."

He hung up and looked down at Addie's chalk-white face. Leaning down, he pressed a quick kiss to her lips. "We'll be okay. But we need to book out of here. Gather snacks and Ollie's insulin. No time for anything else."

She rushed away without a word. It was a good thing Buster had already been fed. They didn't have time to spare. Urgency quickened his movements as he gathered the supplies they might need.

Where could they go? A thought hatched in his mind. Could he go to his parents' house? He disregarded the idea immediately. Now was not the time to risk a reunion.

He completed gathering up what he would need. That included a leash and dog food for Buster.

In the other room, he could hear Addie and Oliver scurrying about. The child didn't complain or ask any questions. Isaiah wondered how Addie had explained the urgent need to skedaddle. Or maybe it spoke to how regular these attacks were becoming. They no longer seemed out of place in the young boy's life.

Someday, Isaiah vowed, they would be able to live without fear. They would have a permanent home and go to sleep at night, never worrying about killers coming in the middle of the night to harm them.

Outside, he heard a motor. A vehicle was coming down the road, slowly, as if it was trying to sneak up on someone. Placing his thumb and index finger under one of the slats of the blinds, Isaiah slowly opened them so the slat moved aside and he could peer out. Sure enough, an unfamiliar Jeep parked on the road, barely visible from the house. Two men exited, their faces half hidden behind winter scarves and their heavy coats. Hats were pulled down around their ears. Either because of the cold or to hide their features. Isaiah was pretty sure it was the second. As they swaggered around the car, he could tell they each carried a gun.

It was time to go.

Racing to the other room, he nearly collided with Addie. She and Ollie were already dressed, and Ollie had a death grip on Buster's collar.

"We need to go now. They're here."

He put the leash on Buster. When the dog started to growl, he gave him the command for silence in German. The growling ceased. Huh. He and Jerry had talked long ago about training dogs to be guard dogs someday. Looks like Jerry took him seriously and did it.

Knowing they couldn't risk the front door, he led them through the mud room and out the back door. He heard the men pounding at the front door. They were trying to break it down. He took two seconds to roll the wheelbarrow outside the screen to the back door. Heaving it up, he wedged it under the door latch so they'd have trouble pushing it open.

It would only slow them down for a moment or two.

Hopefully it would be enough.

Handing Buster's leash to Addie, he picked up Ollie and held him tight. "You'll have to hang on. We need to run. That'll help us go faster." Oliver slid his arms around Isaiah's neck and locked his fingers together.

Isaiah dipped his chin at Addie, indicating he was ready.

She nodded and took off running, Buster at her side. He followed after, his arms closed like steel around the child clinging to his chest. If they shot at him, the boy would still be in danger, but less so than if he were running or riding piggyback.

Footprints. They were leaving footprints.

"Get off the snow, as much as you can."

Addie veered to the left. The snow was patchier here, under the cover of the trees. The ground was so hard that even pounding on it, their feet didn't leave much evidence of their recent passing.

When a shot rang out, followed by the cracking of wood and plastic, he knew what had happened. The hired killers had shot out the doorknob and broken through the back exit. If he lived through this, he'd pay Jerry back for any damage done to his house because he sheltered them from harm.

When Addie slowed and glanced back, a question on her lovely brow, he pointed to the left. They'd head that way. He didn't remember what lay in that direction. But if they headed the other way, they'd have to traipse across the snow again, leaving a trail that was sure to give them away.

It was difficult to tromp silently when haste was the goal. The only positive was that Buster didn't bark and Ollie didn't cry. Both of which would have been natural reactions. Maybe God was watching out for them.

Five minutes later, they halted at the edge of the frozen pond completely blocking their way. On the right, barbed wire fence indicated the property line for the next farm over. Behind them, two hired killers continued their search, loudly thrashing through the snow and bushes. They must have separated.

His gaze met Addie's. The dread in her bright green eyes hardened into steel. She understood.

They had no other option.

Addie swallowed the bile that surged up her esophagus and into her mouth. They were out of choices. If they were to survive this day, she needed to cross that frozen pond.

Now would not be a good time to mention her fear of frozen bodies of water, no matter how small they were. Later, once they were safe and laughing about their adventures, she'd mention it, in a joking, oh-by-the-way kind of story.

Not now.

Now, her only goal was to go across that pond and keep Ollie and Isaiah safe.

The crashing behind her encouraged her to hurry. She stepped out onto the ice. Even knowing it would be slippery, she still wasn't prepared for the way her right leg shot out from beneath her. Only Isaiah's firm grip on her upper arm kept her from face-planting on the cold ice beneath her.

"It's like ice skating," he murmured, his

warm breath caressing her ear. She'd enjoy it so much more if she were not on a layer of frozen water, sure she was going to drown.

"I don't ice skate," she gritted, her teeth clenched so hard her jaw ached from the pressure.

"Okay." He stepped up beside her. "Follow my lead."

They slipped and slid their way across the ice. She started to get the hang of it after the first few minutes. It wasn't anything like roller-skating, but there was a smooth elegance to it, almost like a dance. They were halfway to the other side. She kept her gaze between Ollie and the goal. Hope rose. If they could make it to the other side, they could run again.

A shot rang out.

They'd been found.

Her heartbeat ramped up. Ollie cried. Buster growled and raced back to bite one of the men on the leg. When he screamed and would have injured the dog, Isaiah called the canine back. Buster growled, but whipped around and returned to them.

They had to move faster. She forgot how to move on the ice now that it was double time. Her balance failed. She went down. All right.

She'd crawl. That didn't work either. Isaiah hauled her to her feet, and they pressed on.

One of the men yelled. There was a loud crack. Glancing back over, she saw one down on the ice. The other standing over him, glaring. The situation was obvious. The seated felon had tried to shoot, and the other had clocked him for it. They wrestled. A shot rang out.

They were almost to the other side when she heard it.

The ice was cracking.

One of the villains screamed. His cry was cut off in a gurgle. He'd gone below the ice. The ice was breaking! The fear pummeled her. She could hardly think behind the panic pelting her from inside. They were all going to drown.

"Addie! Keep going. Don't give up."

Isaiah didn't need to remind her. She scooted, an inch at a time, always conscious of where her little boy was. "Don't drop him. He can't swim."

Not only that, but if he got wet, he'd get hypothermia.

When she looked back, her blood chilled as cold as the water below them. The other killer had abandoned his partner and was coming for them. She had no capability to understand the inhumanity behind his actions.

She took another step. As her boot pressed down on the ice, it cracked below her toes. She stepped back. The resulting crack stretched from her current position to the edge of the pond. They were trapped, and the ice was breaking to pieces all around them.

The villain charged at them. Isaiah ripped Ollie from his chest and lofted him gently to Addie. Buster jumped up at the villain, and the man shoved him away and grabbed his gun. When he aimed it at Addie, Isaiah went for him and wrestled him to the cold surface.

They rolled around on the ice for thirty seconds, until Isaiah got an arm free and slammed his fist against the bottom edge of his opponent's jaw. The man's eyes rolled back in his head, and his arms fell slack.

That danger was handled. But how did they get off the ice? It was still too dangerous to run the last few feet.

"We'll have to throw you to the shore."

"What?" She whipped her head to Isaiah. "No way. What about you?"

"I can handle myself on the ice better than you. You'll have to go get help. We'll need a scuba team here to search for the body."

She'd never forget the sight of him going under the ice.

"Please, Addie. Ollie needs to be off the ice."

That was the only reason she agreed. Isaiah picked her up in his arms. "Tuck and roll when you land."

Then she was airborne. Tucking her head, she took the burden of the landing on her legs. Thankfully, the snow cushioned it.

"Send Ollie my way."

She braced herself to receive her son. Ollie, rather than being scared, was delighted when Isaiah tossed him to his mother. It was a perfect throw. She caught him midair, grunting as his weight hit her. Buster began barking and bounded across the ice to land beside his new friend. He didn't weigh enough to break the ice. Ollie wrapped his arms around the dog, who greeted him with slobbery doggie kisses all over his giggling face.

She pivoted to face Isaiah. He wanted her to leave him here. Alone. She had to do it. It was imperative she go and find help. The horror of leaving him to fend for himself slammed into her, leaving her lungs unable to breathe. Her chest hurt.

"Go. Get help."

"Come on, Ollie. We need to go and find someone to get Mr. Isaiah."

Her son frowned, but trustingly put his hand in hers. They hadn't taken more than five steps when Isaiah cried out and a loud snap rent the air.

She whirled around in time to see his body, and that of the unconscious killer, plunge into the icy depths.

TWELVE

"Isaiah!"

Addie charged back to the edge of the pond and dropped to her knees. She landed on a pile of rocks, but she ignored the pain. Stretching out her arms, she dipped her hands beneath the surface, waving them under the water in an attempt to catch his hand, and screamed his name again.

She barely even felt the cold water burning against her skin. Next to her, Ollie cried, calling for Mr. Isaiah.

Two feet away from her, he burst through the surface, gasping, icy water streaming down his hair and face. He struggled to swim the last few feet, dragging something with him.

Someone.

Reaching the shore, he pushed the would-be killer out of the water, thrusting him toward them. The man was barely conscious, but he was alive. She gave him an angry glare, making sure he was no threat, then turned to help Isaiah from the pond. He'd brought a few plants with him, hanging off his shoes, but on the whole, he seemed well.

But he'd freeze if they didn't find a way to warm him up, fast.

There was no way they'd be able to return the way they'd come. There had to be another option.

"Addie. Find help," Isaiah murmured. Then he tipped forward, staggered and collapsed to the ground. He was unconscious before he hit the ground. There was a raw wound on the top of scalp. She recalled hearing a grunt when the second shot had rung out. At the time, she'd been relieved it had missed.

It hadn't.

The bullet had grazed his skull, but he was too stubborn to say anything about it. She put pressure on it, desperate to stop the bleeding. She needed to get them warm. Although saving Isaiah was primary in her mind, she had no desire for the other man to die. He needed to live in order to stand trial for his crimes. Who knew how many others he had killed?

Plus, he might provide crucial information

about the man or woman who wanted them dead so badly.

"Addie!" Jerry's voice yelled out behind her. Buster began barking, leaping and prancing around joyfully as his owner approached.

A sob tore from her mouth. She wasn't alone. She huddled Ollie close to her side and sent up a silent prayer of thanksgiving for sending Jerry. He could help her, Ollie and Isaiah. She refused to consider that it could be too late for Isaiah. He would get better. He had to.

She didn't want to think about living in a world without him in it.

A blanket fell around her shoulders, and another one drifted over Ollie. Jerry hadn't come alone. A second man joined them.

"Isaiah?"

Isaiah's head moved restlessly on the snow. "Scott."

She recognized the name. Jerry's younger brother.

"The neighbor called in hearing shots. The volunteer fire department and an ambulance are on the way," Scott assured him. "We'll get you warm. Who is that man?" He pointed to the outlaw.

New voices intruded. She tensed, scanning the area for the next threat, but relaxed when the Karns brothers both waved the newcomers over. She saw the fire department gear. Help had truly arrived.

What had Scott asked? Oh, he wanted to know about the other man. She waved a hand at the unconscious villain.

"He tried to kill us." Her teeth chattered so much, speaking took effort. "He had a gun. Isaiah's been shot. The bullet scraped his skull."

"Well, I'll be. Lorraine was sure there were two of them." Jerry spat on the ground in a classic sign of contempt.

"There were. The other one fell under the ice into the water. He never came up."

Jerry, Scott and the firemen all fell silent, staring at the now still pond. Shards of ice floated on top. No body was visible. Whoever had fallen in, they weren't coming out alive.

"Charles," the fire chief, easily identifiable by his white helmet, called to one of the other men. "Call 911 and tell them we need the scuba team here. Stat."

The firemen loaded her, Ollie and Isaiah into their vehicles and drove them around the long way to Jerry's house. Smoke still curled out of the chimney. She and Ollie were able to make it inside on their own power. Isaiah had to be carried. After she had checked Ollie's glucose levels, which were shockingly normal, and administered his midday dose of insulin, she set about making tea and hot chocolate for the men swarming around the house.

Isaiah's voice drifted to her. Shutting her lids, she gripped the countertop. She hadn't admitted to herself how afraid she'd been that he'd be taken from her. She swayed for a moment before stiffening her back. She was not the fainting type. He needed her to be strong, and she would be.

He was awake and coherent when she brought him a cup of hot soup. She'd found some chicken noodle soup in the cupboard. It was generic, but she didn't think he'd complain too much. The smile he beamed her way when she entered the room made her stumble and blush. This time, when her pulse thudded in her ears, she couldn't blame it on danger or fear.

It was all his fault. He'd gotten under her skin so fast, it stunned her.

When Jerry snickered, she realized they were staring at each other. She cleared her throat. "Hey. I thought this might make you feel better."

He patted the seat beside him. She handed

him the soup and gingerly sat on the cushion next to him, tucking her leg beneath her.

Isaiah grinned at her then gobbled down his soup. When he had finished, he turned to the men standing around the room. "So, the scuba team came?"

The chief nodded. "Yes. They found a body under the water. He's on his way to the morgue. The other fellow, the one you saved—" she saw the other men murmuring and watching Isaiah with respect "—he's on the way to the hospital. Severe frostbite, but he should live. The police have dispatched an officer to take custody of him there."

"Speaking of the police," one of the men said from the window. "A cruiser just pulled up outside."

She stiffened, wishing they could run. Isaiah's hand found hers. He squeezed it, just like he had the day before in the car. This time, though, he didn't let go, but settled their clasped hands together on the couch between them.

Footsteps clomped up the stairs out front, followed by two hard knocks. Jerry briskly stepped from the room. She heard voices, but couldn't make out the words.

Jerry sounded excited. What was that about?

The first officer entered the room. His gaze slid right past her and fastened on Isaiah. A secret smile played around his lips. When he looked at their joined hands, his smile widened.

She and Isaiah shrugged at each other, confused.

A second man stepped into view. His face was familiar somehow. He didn't wear a police uniform, but he had the bearing of a police officer. When he saw Isaiah, his eyes grew misty. Her mouth dropped open.

Beside her, Isaiah dropped her hand and struggled to his feet. In a voice thick with emotion, he choked out, "Micah!"

Micah reached him in two long strides and pulled him into an embrace. Isaiah wasn't ashamed of the tears coursing down his face. He had feared never seeing his family again, and if he did, he had worried they'd reject him.

Finally, Micah stepped back. His face was wet, as well, although a smile stretched from ear to ear. "I heard my kid brother got himself into some trouble, as usual, so I had to come see what it was."

Joy bubbled up inside. Laughing, Isaiah still managed to pull off a passable scoff. "Me, in trouble! You were the one always landing in scrapes! I was the responsible brother."

"No. That was Gideon."

Both brothers burst into laughter. Gideon had been the worst prankster as a child. He got into more trouble than the other three brothers combined. Zeke was the only one who never added to the chaos in their home.

"Everyone, sit." Jerry and Scott carried some folding chairs into the room.

The volunteer firemen completed their questions and left, now that the police had arrived. Once Micah and the police officer sat, Jerry and Scott sat, too. No one was going to tell Jerry to go to a different room in his own home. Besides, he had earned the right to know what was going on.

"Right. Before we go any further, I need to introduce someone." Micah pointed a finger at the police officer. "This is Sergeant Steve Beck of the Sutter Springs Police Department. He is a fine, upstanding officer of the law. He is also, I am happy to say, our brother-in-law."

It took a moment to sink in. Then he remembered Lorraine saying his sister had married a cop.

"You're Christina—I mean Joss's—husband!" Isaiah held out an eager hand, his gaze swiveling between the two men. "I just learned yesterday she had returned."

Steve shook his hand. The man didn't say anything, but Isaiah didn't care. He couldn't expect him to warm up to a man traveling with a fugitive with a price on her head. Some explanations needed to be made.

Micah apparently felt the same way. He leaned forward and fixed a level stare on his younger brother. "Okay. So, I think we deserve to know some things. Like what happened."

It was time to come clean about everything. He started with Raymond's death. Jerry, Scott and Micah were all dismayed to learn how preventable that death was. "I left and drifted until I decided to enter the military. When I got out, a buddy of mine and I decided to try and make our way as bounty hunters."

The two men weren't impressed with that move, he could see.

"Maybe, if I'd still been at home, I could have helped you through that," Micah mourned.

Isaiah cut that line of thinking off. "Stop. You and I were close, but I had to make my own decisions. And I came to a realization this morning. While I was sitting here getting warm, I understood that if I hadn't left, Addie and Ollie would have been easy prey.

So maybe my leaving was in God's plan all along."

Addie's gorgeous green eyes flared wide. She knew his faith had stumbled. He wanted her to know it was being rekindled.

"That brings up another question," Steve broke in, not unkindly. "She's a fugitive, yet you're helping her."

"She's been set up." When both men raised their eyebrows, he sighed and glanced at her.

"Tell them everything," she said. "They're your family. Don't keep secrets from them."

He grinned at her and winked before turning back to his brothers, for in his mind, Steve was his brother, too, now that he was married to Joss. "It started like this."

He told them about the pictures he'd been sent and about his doubts. When he got to the part about her scar, Steve asked to see it. Lifting one shoulder in a shrug, Addie pulled up her sleeve and showed him the scar. Isaiah flipped through the pictures on his phone and found the correct image. He passed the phone to Steve, glad he'd accidently left it behind when they'd fled the house. If he hadn't, all his evidence would have been ruined when he'd plunged into the pond.

"You're right. It's not the same arm." Steve

passed the phone to Micah. "Not only is the scar wrong, look at her index finger."

The three men crowded around. Micah and Isaiah exclaimed at the same time.

"What?" Addie demanded. "I saw the picture but didn't see anything."

Isaiah took his phone back and moved to sit beside Addie on the couch. He strove to ignore her fragrance and focused on the image. "Hold up your hand."

When she did so, he pointed at her index finger. "Your index finger is shorter than your middle finger. It only comes up to the bottom of your fingernail. Now look at hers."

He held the phone closer. She gasped. "The index and middle finger are the same length!"

"She has a strong resemblance to you," Steve said, smiling. "She could be mistaken for your sister. But the woman in that photo is not Addison Johnson."

Addie sagged back against the couch. "Will Lieutenant Bartlett believe it?"

"Kathy?" Steve frowned. "Why wouldn't she?"

"You haven't talked with her about the case, obviously," Isaiah muttered.

"I just returned home today. I was at court the past three days."

Isaiah shoved his hands through his hair. "She seemed to have her doubts. And we heard that after Officer Yates was shot, the police were after us."

"Let me handle this right now." He pulled his phone out of his pocket and walked to the other room. Isaiah heard him say, "Kathy, I have a story for you…"

Micah locked his attention on Isaiah. "I am assuming you plan to come see *Mamm* and *Daed*?"

It was framed as a question, but he knew it was a command. "Will I be welcome?"

Micah snorted. "Welcome. Brother of mine, you will be overwhelmed with welcome. I'm a deputy US marshal who did his time in the army, and I am greeted with smiles and hugs every time I visit. Not once have they ever reproached me for not joining the church. If I'd left after being baptized, that would have been a different ball of wax. Yes, you will be welcomed."

He turned his warm gaze on Addie. "You and your son will be welcomed, too. *Mamm* loves spoiling babies."

"That she does." Steve rejoined them. "Kathy agrees with my pronouncement that you were framed. She wants to come out tomorrow and talk with you. I am assuming that we'll come to your parents' house. I know Joss will want to see Isaiah, and I think it wise to keep her," he nodded at Addie, "out of town, especially since we have no idea who is coming after her."

Things were moving fast, but Isaiah knew he needed to get it over with, like pulling a bandage off a wound. Do it quick.

"Yeah. We'll meet there."

He hoped Micah was correct that he'd be welcomed home.

THIRTEEN

Micah and Steve insisted on driving Isaiah, Addie and Ollie to the Bender home. Isaiah couldn't decide if his churning stomach was due to excitement or nerves. Probably a combination of both. All he knew was he would never be able to face the embarrassment if he threw up at the thought of seeing his parents again.

He needed a few minutes alone to sort out his feelings and settle his mind. Excusing himself on some flimsy excuse, he headed out to the barn. Inhaling the outdoor scents, his shoulders relaxed.

Nature had always been where he went to clear his mind. Somehow, being inside a house, even if it was quiet, didn't work as well. Right now, Jerry's house was far from a quiet place to think.

He hadn't been outside more than five minutes when Micah joined him. He shouldn't have been surprised. Micah and he had shared a bond when they were kids. No one in the family had understood him the way his oldest brother had. Micah may have been right. Had he been around when Raymond died, Isaiah might not have gone off the deep end the way he did. Although, it worked out for the best in the end.

"Hey. Are you okay?"

He shrugged. "Yeah. I just needed to get my head together. So much has happened in the past few days, it's hard to take in."

"Hmmm." Micah leaned against the wall. "I've missed you. I know you're worried about how *Mamm* and *Daed* will react, but they won't care where you've been. They had five children. At some point, they lost three of them. All they've ever wanted is to have their family back. You're going to make it happen for them."

He hadn't thought of that. "I guess I'm not the only child of theirs that isn't Amish anymore."

"Nope. But they'll love you no matter what."

Isaiah scuffed his toe in the dirt. He went to shove his hands into his pockets then snorted. "I'm not used to not having pockets anymore."

"I'm assuming you are dressed this way as a disguise."

"Yep."

"Will you give it up now that you've been found?"

He shook his head. "As far as I can tell, only those two who came after us today know about the Amish garb. They're both taken care of. The trouble is, both Addie and my pictures are being circulated out there now. I don't want anyone other than those here now to know I've returned. As far as the town of Sutter Springs knows, I'm still out in the wild."

"Now that Addie no longer has to worry about the police coming for her, hopefully this will be solved soon." Micah straightened. "I'll let you alone to think in a minute. Just one more question. What's going on with you and Addie?"

"Truth? I have no idea. I have feelings for her. But I'm a bit messed up right now. Lot to think through and consider."

"I know the feeling." Micah punched him in the shoulder and departed, letting the door swing closed behind him.

Isaiah sighed. He may as well face the music sooner rather than later. He pivoted on his heel to head inside. The door cracked open again, and Addie crept into the barn. His heart warmed. Her eyes were full of concern for him. He hadn't had someone care about him for so long, and now it seemed he was overwhelmed with people who wanted to help him.

"Hey. It's cold in here." He grinned at her.

"I can see that. I'm wearing a coat." She stepped closer. He could feel her warm breath hitting his chin. "I was hoping you were all right. No effects from being in the pond this afternoon?"

He let a wry chuckle slide through his teeth. "No effects from the dunking that I'm aware of. All the family coming out of the woodwork, now, well that's a different story."

She peered up at him. "You're happy, though, right?"

He nodded. "Yeah. I am. But I'm wondering what seeing my folks will bring."

"Well, it might not matter much, but Ollie and I will be there with you."

Her gaze slid away, as if she was embarrassed at her words. He placed his fingers under her chin and tilted her head up so he could see her face. "If anything could make it better, that would do it."

Without planning it, he leaned down and placed a careful kiss on her lips. She smiled.

He didn't dare kiss her again. It was becoming a habit.

"We'll be leaving in a few moments."

"I'm done here. Lead the way." Interlacing their fingers together, he walked back to the house with her.

Oliver wasn't impressed with the plan to leave again so soon. "I don't want to go somewhere else. I want to stay with Buster."

No matter what Addie said, he didn't want to hear it. Isaiah decided to try. He squatted down to Ollie's eye level. "Son, you're making your mother sad."

Ollie raised a stricken face to him. "I don't want to do that. I love my mommy."

His chest felt constricted. The kid was killing him. "I understand. Can I tell you a secret?"

Ollie nodded, clutching his stuffed dog close to his chest.

Isaiah took a deep breath. He could feel the gazes of everyone in the room centered on them. He knew what he needed to say. He just wished it wasn't being said so publicly. He swallowed back his pride. If it would help Ollie, and by extension, Addie, he'd live through it. "I once made my mommy really sad, too."

The little boy's green eyes, so like his mother's, widened. "You did, Mr. Isaiah?"

He nodded. "I did. She's been sad for a really long time. I need to go see her to fix that."

"Are you going to take her sad away?"

He smiled, his insides melting at the sweetness of the child. "Yes. That's why we're going."

Ollie reached out and patted his face. "We need to make your mommy happy."

"Will you go? Without arguing?"

For an answer, Ollie suddenly leaned forward and looped his small arms around Isaiah's neck. He gently embraced Ollie back. Raising his gaze, he found Addie's tear-filled one.

"Thank you." She mouthed, smiling. He'd do a lot for her smile.

When he stood, he gathered Ollie's hand in his and led him out to the car. Micah wordlessly clapped his hand on Isaiah's shoulder before he got into the passenger seat of Steve's cruiser. Addie slid in behind Steve, and Isaiah would sit behind Micah. Ollie's booster seat was placed between them.

During the silent car ride, Isaiah watched the scenery fly past. Some of it was familiar. Other things were new. "This area has been built up a lot."

"It has. That's progress." There was a note in Micah's voice suggesting he really didn't like all the progress. There was nothing to be done about it.

If only he could sit beside Addie. He wanted to hold her hand, like he'd done before. That wouldn't be possible with their seating arrangement without drawing undue attention to it.

When the car turned onto his parents' road, he sat up straighter in his seat. Time seemed to slow down as they cruised down the road. The familiar houses sent an ache rushing through him. The houses owned by Englisch had vehicles in the driveway, Christmas decorations dotting the yards and Christmas trees framed in the windows. One place had a political sign from the past election in their yard.

And then they were there. Steve flashed his blinker briefly before steering into the driveway and rolling up toward the large white farmhouse. Beyond the farmhouse, the barn that had been there since before Isaiah was born greeted him like an old friend. The buggy the family used was visible under its roof. His *daed's* workshop stood off to the side.

It was like he never left.

Silently, he exited the vehicle and stood staring up at the house. Addie and Ollie moved to his side. Ollie took his hand. Smiling down at the little boy, he slowly made his way to the back door and followed Steve and Micah into the house.

"Steve! Micah!" his mother's voice, just as he recalled it, greeted his brothers. "I didn't know you were coming. Who—"

Her voice sputtered to a stop as Isaiah stepped across the threshold of his childhood home. Tears swam in her eyes as she gazed into his face.

Before he could make a sound, she was there, her arms around him. "Isaiah!"

"Hi, *Mamm*. I'm home."

Addie eased into the spacious kitchen behind Isaiah and stood to the side, Ollie silent at her side. She blinked back the emotion clouding her vision and watched the family drama unrolling before her. Steve stood near the counter, and Micah slipped through the door to go deeper into the house. She could hear the low rumble of male voices.

And then an older man who could only be the family patriarch entered the room. He approached his wife and long-lost offspring, tears unashamedly streaming into his dark beard, heavily threaded with grey. Behind him, Micah stood, stoic except for the telltale moisture in his eyes. When Edith Bender stepped back, Nathan took her place.

"*Daed.*" Isaiah's gravelly voice held extra grit. He was hanging on to his composure by a thread. "Forgive me."

"My *sohn*, there's nothing to forgive."

Ollie tugged at Addie's hand. "Is Mr. Isaiah's mom still sad, Mommy?"

Addie flushed as everyone's attention shifted to her and the child at her side.

"Isaiah, is this your wife and *sohn*?" Edith Bender asked.

Then the woman gazed at Isaiah's clean-shaven jaw, her confusion clear. Suddenly, Addie remembered something she'd heard. Amish men grew a beard once they were married and wore it for the rest of their lives. Although he was dressed in Amish clothes and had arrived with her and Ollie in tow, Isaiah was obviously not a married man.

Awkward. She shifted on her feet. Isaiah grinned. It was the happy grin of a man who'd found his way back. "Nah. She's someone special I'm helping."

Someone special. She liked the way that sounded.

"Is she Plain?" His mother frowned.

"No. I'm sorry, *Mamm*. I never joined the church. I—"

"I think we should *cumme* into the *haus* and make ourselves comfortable," she said, interrupting him. "Isaiah, *cumme*. You are back. That's what's important."

The slight accent she'd sometimes heard in his voice came through loud and clear in his parents' voices. Within two minutes, she found herself sitting in a comfortable room with Isaiah's family, a glass of water in her hand. Isaiah gratefully accepted the mug of steaming black coffee his mother handed him, taking a sip and smacking his lips.

Addie quirked an eyebrow at him.

"It's real. Not instant." He took a second, slower sip, savoring the taste. She held back a chuckle. She had seen his distaste when Jerry offered him instant coffee or tea.

While Isaiah rehashed both his history and her current situation with his family, she noticed Steve murmuring to Micah. When Micah nodded vehemently, Steve left quietly. She heard the back door close a minute before she heard his car start. From her seat, she had a view of the road and watched the cruiser leave the driveway. Where was Steve going?

The rest of the family didn't remark on his

smooth exit. She returned her focus to Isaiah. When he got to the part about the men chasing them at Jerry's place, his mother's hand flew to her throat.

"I'll understand if you don't want me here," Addie said when there was a break in the conversation. "I don't want to bring danger to your family."

"Nee." Nathan smiled at her, his face kind. "You were the means *Gott* used to bring our *sohn* home. We are grateful. *Gott* has a plan. He is in control. You are always *welkum* here."

Ten minutes later, Steve's cruiser returned. She could see other people were in the vehicle and had an inkling of who he'd gone to fetch. Her intuition was proved correct when the back door slammed and running feet tore through the kitchen and into the living room.

Two young men, one bearded, one fresh-faced, but obviously related based on their similar features, slammed to a halt inside the door, standing as if their boots were nailed to the floor, and stared at Isaiah. He rose to his feet, jaw working, as he faced his brothers. He took a single step toward them, breaking them from the emotion that held them there.

"Isaiah!" They both yelled. The three brothers

met in a clash of arms and back thumps. Laughter rolled through the room.

Movement at the door caught her attention. A lovely young woman with blond hair neatly tucked beneath a *kapp* watched the reunion, joy stamped on her face.

"Molly," the bearded man reached out a hand to her, his voice filled with so much love Addie caught her breath. The woman gripped his hand and moved to his side with a slight limp. "Molly. This is my brother. Isaiah, I don't know if you remember, but we grew up with the Schultz family."

"Ah! I heard you and Zeke had gotten married. Congratulations!"

"*Denke*. Our *kinder* are with my mother. We have twins."

That meant the other brother had to be Gideon. The prankster. Looking at his dancing eyes, she could definitely see the mischief lurking in their depths. Isaiah introduced her to his brothers. They accepted her and Ollie without question, the same as his parents had. Not all families would have done so, she knew, regardless of whether they were Amish or not. She couldn't be blind to the fact that she represented a very real danger to them.

Yet they trusted God would provide.

The day hadn't finished with its surprises. An hour after they arrived, two more vehicles pulled into the driveway. Soon the house rang with the laughter of children. Two more women were introduced to her. Lissa, Micah's wife entered with a young daughter a couple years older than Ollie and an infant son. Ollie was immediately entranced by the daughter, Shelby.

When the second woman entered, her little girl immediately got swept up in Edith Bender's embrace. Steve took the young boy from the woman's arms and greeted her with a kiss.

This was Joss, the sister who'd been abducted. Isaiah broke away from his brothers and held open his arms. Joss ran to him. The room stilled. Several people sniffed, but she couldn't tear her gaze from the scene to see who.

"Our whole family," Edith said to her husband. "They've all *cumme* home."

"Ja." He cleared his throat. *"Gott* is very *gut."*

The family rearranged to make room for everyone. Gideon and Zeke opted to sit on the floor with the children, and soon both of them had little ones clinging to them and tumbling into their laps. Addie had thought to move off the couch and let someone else have her place near Isaiah. He had vetoed the idea the moment she began to move, grabbing her hand and silently asking her to stay. Pleased, she subsided and remained at his side. Joss claimed the cushion on his other side.

An alarm buzzed on her phone. Feeling conspicuous pulling out the device in an Amish home, she peered at it as discreetly as she could.

"Everything all right?"

Isaiah's question brought immediate silence. Unnerved by the sudden attention, she shook her head and showed him the numbers.

He stood and waved to Ollie. "This young man needs some juice. *Mamm,* is it all right if we raid the ice box?"

"*Ja,* of course." Worry clouded her voice. "What's wrong? Can I help?"

Addie stood. "It's fine. Ollie has diabetes, and his glucose numbers are low. He'll have some juice and be fine."

The older woman put her hand on her husband's leg and pushed herself to her feet. "*Ack.* I should get dinner on the table. It will be a quick meal. What we have ready."

Joss and Molly both joined them to help out. Within half an hour, a satisfying meal had been served.

She'd always thought Amish meals would be solemn affairs. No gathering, she soon decided, could be solemn with all the Bender siblings in one place. Zeke was definitely the quietest brother, but his reticence was more than made up for by the boisterous Gideon. Micah, she discovered, appeared sober and somewhat intimidating, but his calm facade hid a dry sense of humor.

It was the most enjoyable meal she'd had in a very long time.

By the time Joss and Zeke took their families home, she felt as if she'd been among them forever. Gideon still lived with his parents as the youngest son. He also, she discovered, worked with his father in the carpentry shop. Zeke owned his own farrier business.

Edith prepared a room for Addie and Ollie to sleep in. She didn't think she'd be able to sleep after the events of the day, but weariness pulled her under within minutes of her head hitting the pillow. When she woke, the morning sun was beginning to stream through the windows. Ollie was curled against her side.

She kissed his head and left the bed to dress and get ready. She had no idea what the day would bring, but she wanted to be prepared to act. Ollie was awake by the time she was finished. After he'd been dressed and his face washed, they joined the family downstairs.

Isaiah met her at the kitchen door.

The intensity of his gaze told her something had already happened.

"What?"

"I got a call this morning from my buddy Henry."

She tensed. He'd asked Henry to do some detective work, if she recalled right. "And?"

"He found something and needs to see us both."

FOURTEEN

"You go. I'll watch Ollie," Edith Bender insisted.

Could she do it? Could she go with Isaiah and leave her son with his parents? Isaiah's friend had said he needed Addie to see something, so she had to go with him. But leave Ollie?

Isaiah hung up the phone. "Micah is on his way here. He will stay with the family while we're gone. And Steve's coming to give us a ride."

Henry had told them to meet him in town. He'd left his place early that morning and had called once he arrived in Sutter Springs. Isaiah hadn't wanted to meet in public, so they had agreed on an old, abandoned office building twenty minutes away.

She finally agreed. Micah would be able to

protect both his parents and her child. She would never forgive herself if any of them came to harm because of her.

Micah pulled in five minutes after Steve arrived. Isaiah's parents said nothing about the gun slipped into his waistband, although she could tell they didn't approve. He hugged his mother while she had a quiet talk with Ollie about her expectations for his behavior.

"I'll be good, Mommy," he declared. "Isaiah's mommy is nice."

She smiled, ruffling his hair. His parents were kind. More so than she'd expected them to be, considering all the baggage she'd dropped like a ticking bomb in their midst. When Isaiah called out to her, she gave Ollie a final kiss on the cheek, thanked Edith then met Isaiah at the cruiser outside. Isaiah, true gentleman that he was, held the back door open for her. When she folded herself into the back seat, he closed the door then joined Steve in the front.

"Now I really feel like a fugitive," she groused, amused.

"Sorry, Addie." Steve grinned at her. "I need him up here so we can get all our plans laid out."

She waved a hand at him. "I was only kidding."

Isaiah looked back over his shoulder at her. "I'd rather sit back there with you than up here with this guy."

She laughed, knowing that he already regarded his sister's husband with affection.

Her amusement faded the closer they drew to town. She pressed a fist into her stomach to still the trembling. Only yesterday, they'd come close to being killed. She knew Henry, but not well. Still, Isaiah had survived in a high danger career for years. He wouldn't trust just anybody. And she knew he'd served with Henry.

It was the rest of the people around them that were the threat. Each time they passed a vehicle on the road, she flinched away from their gazes. Was a potential killer in that car, coming for her?

Stop it, she ordered herself. All she was doing was making herself ill with this conjecture. Gritting her teeth, she bowed her head and prayed for guidance and protection. When both Isaiah and Steve said "Amen," her head jerked up. She hadn't realized she'd been praying out loud.

Steve and Isaiah kept up a low conversation ahead of her. She tuned it out. Her eyes scoured the snowy landscape. When nothing worrisome popped out at her, she sank back into the seat and allowed her mind to drift.

"This is it," Isaiah said.

Addie leaned forward and peered out the window. It didn't look like much. The building looked like it had once been part of a chain convenience store. All the front windows and the door had been boarded up, reminding her of images she'd seen of people preparing for a hurricane.

"Are you sure?" Steve frowned, eyeing the place with distaste. He hesitated at the entrance. "It doesn't look like anyone else is here."

"I'm sure. He must be delayed. Ah." He pointed out the window. There was another entrance on the other side of the lot. "That's his truck now."

Henry drove into the parking lot and parked next to the building.

"Okay. Let's do this." Steve pulled into the parking lot.

Henry left his vehicle and stood at the tailgate, waiting.

A sedan spun around the corner and

screeched to a halt. Before Isaiah could shout a warning to Henry, the barrel of a gun was shoved out the window and two shots rang out. Henry's body jerked twice then fell to the ground.

Steve slammed the cruiser into Park and lowered his window. Addie hadn't seen him pull his gun. He was that fast. The gun that had taken Henry down re-aimed, pointing in their direction. Steve fired. The front window shattered. The gun dropped to the street. The sedan drifted forward, stopping when it hit the curb.

Isaiah and Steve both exited the cruiser.

"Stay here!" Isaiah barked at her.

He ran across the parking lot to his friend, while Steve ran to the sedan. She watched as the man she'd grown to care for dropped to his knees beside his friend and checked him for life signs. She slumped back, drained.

A sudden thump at her window made her jump. Another man, grinning at her, waved bye-bye before aiming a gun at her face.

Steve shouted. Isaiah spun away from his injured friend in time to see the second gunman aiming for his Addie.

Without pause, he hooked his hand around his Glock and brought it up, firing to disable the villain. The would-be villain howled and fell to the ground, holding on to his knee. He would not be standing on that leg anytime soon.

Steve ran over to deal with the live shooter. He must have been sitting in wait. Somehow, they'd followed Henry. Fortunately, Henry had been smart and worn a Kevlar vest. It had taken the bullet that would have struck his heart. It was the bullet that had pierced his shoulder Isaiah was worried about.

Glancing over his shoulder, he saw the gunman was completely subdued. Steve was on the phone. The back door opened and Addie got out, avoiding getting near the man who'd tried to kill her. She ran across the lot, the green dress flapping against her legs, not stopping until she reached his side.

"Will he be all right?"

"I think so."

Henry groaned.

"What about you?" Isaiah didn't know how he'd deal with it if he lost her. Not now.

"I'm perfect." She gave him a tight smile. "You saved my life back there."

"I don't want to ever see anyone pointing a gun at you again. I thought my heart would stop."

She touched his face. "I'm good. And I hope the same thing. Here."

She shoved a blanket she'd grabbed from the back seat at him. He took it and used it to press against Henry's shoulder in an attempt to stem the red blood flowing freely from the gunshot wound.

By the time the two ambulances arrived, Addie was shivering, probably from a delayed reaction. He stood and wrapped his arms around her while the paramedics tended his friend. "Let's get you back to the cruiser. Steve can drop us off at the hospital."

Steve had called for the coroner, as well as for another officer to meet them at the hospital to take charge of the wounded prisoner. Addie didn't protest, either to being in his arms or to the escort back to Steve's cruiser. Isaiah was all too aware of how perfectly she fit nestled beneath his chin. It was as if they were made to fit together.

Except he still had issues. And a job that could be hazardous. Not to mention someone was still out to see her, and now him, dead. Yeah, there were a few kinks to work out if they were ever to have any kind of future together.

Once at the hospital, Isaiah got them both

some hot coffee before they settled into the uncomfortable chairs in the waiting area.

"What about Ollie?" she asked.

"Micah knows what to do," he assured her. "I talked with him last night. His boss's daughter has type 1 diabetes. He has him on speed dial if he needs any more information and can't get ahold of you. Why don't you give him a quick call, if you're worried?" He rattled off Micah's number.

"Will he answer a strange number?"

"I gave him yours last night, in case there was ever an emergency. I meant to plug his into your phone, but you went to bed before we came back in from the barn."

They'd gone to the barn to talk privately about the current situation.

Since she didn't say anything but dialed the number he gave her, he decided she wasn't mad about his presumption. When she hung up, the tightness in her shoulders eased.

It was close to one in the afternoon before they were allowed into the recovery room to see Henry. His friend was pale and groggy, but still coherent.

"Hey. I thought you were done for," Isaiah said.

Addie winced at the comment, but Henry

grinned. They had seen so much together, neither of them bothered to hold back what they thought. Henry was one person he could always count on to tell him the unvarnished truth. He hadn't realized until this moment how precious that kind of friendship was.

"Not my time." He coughed once. "I have some intel for you."

Isaiah nodded, pulling a chair closer to the bed for Addie to sit in. "Yeah? You said you had some interesting news."

"Chad Whitman? The man who hired you? He was murdered two days ago."

That was unexpected. And sad. "So, he really did hire me?"

"He did. But then the Sutter Springs department, namely Officer Alan Yates, got involved. He sent information showing that Addison Bruce Johnson had alibis for certain times under question. Unfortunately, he was injured before he could talk with Whitman personally. Regardless, Whitman took the info and contacted the appropriate people. When the Pennsylvania State Police and district attorney got their hands on this new information, they did some digging. Whatever they found convinced them, and the charges against Addie were dropped. When they tried to contact Whitman, they discovered he'd been pushed in front of a train."

Addie gasped. "How awful."

"It is that. It seems that Whitman was not the person who put a hit out on Addie."

"Who was?" He was surprised by this new intel. In fact, he'd been almost positive that the person he'd been contracted by and the person who had put a price on Addie's head were one and the same. Thinking about it now, he wondered if the person who wanted her dead had grown impatient waiting for him to find her and had put out the contract.

"A witness saw the murder. She identified this man as the one who pushed Whitman." Groaning, he stretched out his hand and grabbed his cell phone. He scrolled through until he found an image. "Addie, does this man look familiar?"

Her hand covered her mouth, her eyes wide with horror. "It looks almost like my husband. But he's been dead for years."

Shocked, he glanced at the picture before switching to the internet and typing her husband's name into the search bar. When the image of her late husband in his uniform appeared, along with articles about his death, he whistled. The man who had pushed Chad hadn't been William Johnson. But he sure could have been his stunt double.

That was no coincidence.

FIFTEEN

Addie's stomach plummeted. She stared at the image on Henry's phone. "It's not Bill. I know it's not. The face is slightly longer. The lips are thinner. But at a quick glance, it looks like him."

She turned to Isaiah. "I don't understand what this means."

He looped his arm over her shoulders, tugging her close to his side. She leaned in, absorbing the warmth and comfort he promised. "I don't have answers yet, Addie. But I will keep looking. My first guess is he is a relative of some kind."

She shook her head. "It's a lot to take in. That my husband might have family. But why would they want me dead?"

"Another question is why would they want your husband dead?" Her head whipped around to the door.

Steve entered the room, followed by Lieutenant Bartlett. "What?"

"Officer Yates is going to be fine. He's out of danger and anxious to get back to work," Lieutenant Bartlett said. "He also has the image of the suspect. It went out to all the precincts in the area. Being the smart guy that he is, he also searched the records of your husband's death. This morning, at his request, I took the image to the witnesses of your husband's shooting. While he didn't shoot him himself, the witness saw the image and remembered seeing him walk away from the scene of the shooting."

"The man who shot my husband was never found," she said through stiff lips.

"We believe he was. The body of a well-known criminal who killed for money was found later that same day near the scene. He was poisoned. It can't be proven now, but my gut tells me he was the one who pulled the trigger."

And then he was disposed of. The way one would throw out a plastic fork once the meal was done. The cavalier treatment of life astonished her. Nausea rolled through her stomach. She pressed her hand to it, trying to calm its motion.

Isaiah spoke for a few more minutes with the police. He kept glancing her way, checking on her. She forced a smile, wanting to reassure him. He didn't seem impressed.

"Hold on, honey," he murmured as they left Henry's room and headed out to the car. "I will get you back to my folks' house. We can make sure Ollie didn't cause any mischief and plan our next move."

She didn't trust herself to speak, so she settled for taking his hand and holding on. When he pressed her fingers, she blinked back the moisture in her eyes. How would she get through this if he wasn't at her side?

Which was a moot question. He was here. She and Ollie were safe. The police were aware of the danger, and they had a suspect in mind. The likelihood of a positive outcome had increased a hundredfold since they were nearly killed at the pond.

Yet, she couldn't stop shaking. So many close calls. Too many people out to get her. For money. That bothered her as much as the rest. That someone would willingly murder to gain wealth. She couldn't comprehend that level of malice.

Once they arrived at the Bender home, Addie leaped from the car and raced inside the house, desperate to hold her son and verify all was well. Inside the house, she heard shrieking laughter.

Lissa had stopped by with her children.

Shelby and Ollie sat side by side, looking through some picture books together. Even as she watched, the older child sneaked in a strategic tickle. Ollie shrieked, moving his arms to protect his ticklish belly. A second later, he launched a counterattack. The two dissolved into giggles. All was well.

For the remainder of the day, Addie's nerves were on pins and needles. Every time she saw Isaiah on his phone, her gut clenched. Would this be the moment they were attacked again? When the attack she expected didn't come, she'd relax, but never completely.

"I keep waiting for something to happen," she confided to Edith.

The older woman reached over and patted her hand. "*Gott* will help you. Lay all your burdens on Him."

It was solid advice. She knew it was. But it wasn't as easy to accomplish as she'd always thought. Addie grimaced. She'd always believed she trusted God with her life. Now she needed to put it into practice.

Sleep evaded her that night. When she woke up the next morning, she stumbled around for a few minutes before Isaiah handed her a cup of coffee. "It's full octane."

"Good. The last thing I need right now is decaf."

"Rough night?"

"Understatement. I couldn't sleep."

He nodded. "I get it. Sometimes, I'm so tired, but my mind won't stop running."

She shifted until they stood shoulder to shoulder against the countertop. "It's annoying. I can't do this too many nights."

"We'll find him, Addie."

He understood her so well. She twisted toward him and kissed his cheek. When he quirked his brows, she smiled her thanks and focused on the hot mug of caffeinated goodness in her hand.

She gulped it down and went for another cup. This one, she sipped slowly.

The morning dragged by. After lunch, she put Ollie down for a nap. He was getting cranky. He complained that he didn't want to sleep, but then fell asleep while she rubbed his back. Edith met her in the hall.

"I need to go to the store. Nathan is taking me in the buggy. Will you be all right here with only Isaiah?"

"Absolutely!"

She didn't want them to think they couldn't live their lives because she was here.

Steve showed up after they left. The moment she saw him walk through the door, she knew he had news.

"Meet Robert Johnson, Jr.," he announced, setting a printed photo on the table. It was the man Henry had shown her on his phone.

"Johnson! I know it's a common name, but he is related to my late husband, am I right?"

"He is. In fact, he's his older brother. By about four minutes."

She kept her countenance by a mere thread. "A twin? My husband had a twin brother?"

"Yep. He was raised by his dad in Seattle. Not sure why. I don't have all the facts yet. What I do know is that he was spotted at the mall an hour ago."

"What are we waiting for?" Isaiah paced the room. "Can we get him?"

"Security is watching him." Steve folded the paper and put the photo back in his pocket. "I'm meeting Lieutenant Bartlett there. She might already have him in her sights. Hang tight here."

"Go," she told him. "I won't rest until he's in jail."

Steve departed. She melted into Isaiah's arms. "It's almost over."

"It will be soon." He pulled back and dropped

a kiss on her forehead. "Look, I know you're tired. Why don't you try to nap while Ollie is down? I want to go out to *Daed's* workshop and clean my gun in case I need it."

She was exhausted. The idea of a nap appealed to her like never before.

She went up to the room, intent on getting some sleep. Ollie, however, had taken over the entire bed. Smiling, she brushed his curls off his forehead. Her little man. She'd try and rest on the couch in the front room.

The only problem was the front room was way too bright. The sunlight streamed into the window, and there were no curtains or blinds to cut down the glare. She stood in front of the glass and looked out. From her vantage point, she had a clear view of the houses directly across the road. They were obviously not Amish. Christmas decorations covered the entire front lawn of one house. Everything from lights and figurines to an oversize blow-up snowman. The house beside it had more understated decorations. The Christmas tree in the picture window was the most extravagant part.

Suddenly, she missed her home. Not the house, exactly, but being in her own space, not a visitor in someone else's.

A movement distracted her. A man moved toward the window. Horrified, she found herself staring into the eyes of Robert Johnson.

She turned to flee as he raised his arm. She saw a flash of silver a moment before he flung something through the glass window. It shattered.

The canister smashed against the hardwood floor, hissing and spewing a colorless gas in the air. It carried the strong scent of pepper. Addie's lungs and throat burned, and her eyes burned. Tugging her apron over her mouth, she fought against the urge to cough and choke on the tear gas.

Ollie! He was still napping.

Spinning away from the window, she dashed through the house and charged into the room. Her son was crying for her on his bed. She gathered him to her chest, ran from the room and lumbered out the back door and down the steps.

Another man appeared at her side and ripped Ollie from her arms. His stuffed dog fell to the ground. Robert stepped on the dog then hooked his hand around her bicep. "We don't need the kid."

She opened her mouth to scream. He clamped his hand over it.

Ollie reacted. He opened his mouth wide

and bit the hand holding him, drawing blood. Swearing, the killer dropped him. Ollie fell and rolled to his feet.

Addie kicked the heel of her boot into Robert's shin. He evidently wasn't used to doing the dirty work himself. Her move not only shocked him, he released his hold. She grabbed her child in her arms and took off. She couldn't head to the workshop where Isaiah was. Robert was blocking her path.

She took off down the road, screaming for help.

She couldn't run that far, not holding Ollie. She had to find cover. She ducked behind a cover of trees.

Still, she kept running. Feet pounded after her. The gunman or Robert? Both would kill her and Ollie without a second thought. She had to find a way out. If only she hadn't left her phone in the house. She could have called 911.

But she was out in the woods with her diabetic child with no phone. And, her blood chilled, no diabetic kit. Ollie should be getting close to needing a snack. If she didn't get him to safety, she ran the very real risk of having him go into a diabetic emergency.

A shot rang out. It missed her by a mile. Ha. It must have been Robert after her. Surely, a trained killer would have come closer. A bright spark of hope ignited in her soul. If she could hold out against Robert, it would give Isaiah time to find her.

A second shot. This one was too close. It brushed her arm, stinging.

"Mommy," Ollie whimpered when he saw the blood.

"It's all right baby. It's a scratch. Nothing to worry about. We've got to keep moving."

She might have made it if she'd seen the branch hidden beneath a pile of snow-covered leaves. Her toes hooked around it, and her ankle wrenched. As she fell, she saw Ollie tumble. She tried to stand. White hot agony seared through her. It was broken or badly sprained. Either way, she couldn't walk on it. And she could hear him coming.

Ollie was crying. "Ollie, I need you to be brave. You have to go find Mr. Isaiah. Go find him and tell him I need him."

He didn't want to go, but she had raised her son to obey her. He turned and fled. She might die, but maybe her child would survive. It was enough.

Isaiah completed cleaning his gun and went to collect his phone. He'd been charging it at the electrical outlet while he worked. The Amish weren't allowed electricity in their homes, but they could sometimes have it approved for inside their businesses.

When he picked up the device, he saw he had several notifications. He hadn't heard the phone ring. He listened to the message with growing alarm. Robert Johnson had slipped through the mall security. He was at large.

Instinct told Isaiah he would try to come here. They should have moved on.

Grabbing his gun, he lurched for the workshop door. Outside, he nearly collided with a stranger standing in the middle of the yard. The stranger looked at Isaiah and grinned. When his hand reached back, Isaiah reacted.

He brought his gun out and shot. The man yelled and grabbed onto his arm, the yellow fabric of his jacket stained with blood. It wasn't a bad wound. He knew he'd barely nicked the man. It had been just enough to cause him to drop the gun.

Micah pulled into the drive. Relief coursed through Isaiah's blood. He couldn't let the gunman go, but he had to find Addie and Ollie.

His older brother jumped from his SUV and ran toward them. "Steve called. Is this him?"

He shook his head. "Another random hit-man, trying to collect an illegal reward."

The man barked out an ugly laugh and sneered. "Not so random. Your girl and her kid, though, they won't be any more trouble."

A red haze filled his mind. Micah had to yell before he could hear through it. "Isaiah! Go see if you can find them. Search the house."

Keeping his weapon ready, he rushed through the back door, calling for Addie and Ollie. No response. Heavy fumes threatened to overwhelm him. He backed out of the house. Micah might have a mask to protect against the vapors. His brother was loading the gunman into the back of his SUV. There was something on the ground, squished into the snow.

Heart racing so hard it felt like it would leap clean out of his chest, he bent down and grabbed the item.

Bowie.

Ollie would never leave his beloved toy behind, not if he had a choice. "We have to find them," he said to Micah.

"Let's get a search party going."

Micah called 911, while Isaiah called Jerry. "Get everyone you can down here. Addie and Ollie are missing."

He didn't wait for the aid to show up. If

things were serious enough that Ollie left his dog behind, he feared the glucose kit had been left behind as well. Micah had an apple sitting in the front console of his car. Reaching in, Isaiah snagged it, knowing his brother would give his all to save a child. And that apple just might save his life.

"Help is on the way!" Micah called.

Isaiah waved to show he heard him. "They can join me in progress."

He had to find the woman he loved and the boy who was like his son before it was too late. Nothing else mattered.

SIXTEEN

He hadn't gone far when he heard a voice that nearly brought him to his knees.

"Mr. Isaiah!" Ollie shrieked. His face was scratched from branches. Tears streaked his face and his nose ran, but he was alive. "Mr. Isaiah. Mommy told me to find you. She's hurt. A bad man chased us. He shot Mommy, and her leg hurts."

Isaiah swallowed back the bile surging up his throat. She wasn't dead. He would find her. "Okay, son. We'll find her."

The little boy was pale and shaking. His lips had a bluish tinge, and he swayed on his feet. Recognizing the signs of low glucose, Isaiah sent a prayer upward, thanking God for providing in this desperate situation. He handed the boy the apple and demanded that he eat it.

Then he handed him the dog. "Let's go."

If he had his druthers, he'd send him back to the Bender house. However, that obviously wasn't an option at the moment. They trudged through the woods for what seemed like forever.

A spot of red on the snow made his stomach plummet to his feet. He knelt next to the splotch, ignoring his damp knees, and touched it. It was blood. Recent blood. It still dripped from his fingers.

Ollie had told him she'd been shot. "Ollie," he kept his voice calm and steady with an effort. "You said your mommy had been shot."

"She was! She carried me, and when the bad man shot her, she dropped me."

"Where was she shot? What part of her body?" He clenched his fists while awaiting the answer.

Ollie touched his fingers to the top of his arm. "Here. She said it was not a bad hurt."

Any mother would have said the same. "Are you sure it wasn't here?"

He touched his shoulder.

Ollie shook his head, adamant. "Nope. Not there. I saw the blood on her arm."

That was good. If he'd hit her shoulder, he could have nicked her artery. Although no bullet wound was a good one, if it had been just a scrape on the top of her arm, she should be okay. Provided she got medical treatment soon.

In the distance ahead, he could hear something thrashing around. It could have been an animal. Or it could have been a person. Signaling Ollie to keep back, he moved forward.

That was when he saw her. Addie. His Addie was leaned up against a tree, her face a mask of pain. Her arm was stained with blood, but it wasn't as bad as he'd feared.

An angry yell startled him. She blanched and flinched, trying to move away as a man lunged at her. He grabbed her, his hand closing on her wounded arm. She screamed in pain.

"Since no one else can take care of you, I'll do it myself!" he growled at her.

Not on his watch. Isaiah charged at the man. "Drop her, Johnson."

Robert Johnson looked at the determined bounty hunter almost upon him and paled. "No!" He grabbed for a gun, fumbled with it. His unsteady hands aimed right at Isaiah.

Isaiah didn't even bother to aim his gun. He kicked out, knocking the gun from Robert Johnson's hands. The man howled. Not so much with pain as with rage. Isaiah bowled him over. He hit the ground, unconscious. Feeling Johnson's neck, Isaiah assured himself that the man was still breathing, then he went to Addie.

He didn't like her color. She'd lost too much blood. Although not as bad as it could have been, the wound continued to bleed. He tore off a strip of his shirt and used it to bind the injury. She blinked, her pain-filled eyes hazy. She wasn't going to stay conscious much longer.

"Argh!"

Johnson. Isaiah spun on his heel. Johnson pulled a long, wicked-looking knife out of a bag sitting amidst the foliage. With a gleeful grin, he raised it above his head and charged. As he drew close to Addie, his arm plunged downward. The blow would kill instantly if it landed.

Isaiah yanked his gun up and fired. The bullet knocked Robert Johnson back. He staggered and fell. He didn't rise again.

He'd killed him. He knew it even before he checked for a pulse. He had never killed before. Had never wanted to. But now he had. It was the only way to save the lives of the two people he loved most in the world.

"Mommy!"

Oliver tumbled toward her. Addie lifted her arms and caught him, falling back against the tree as he hit her in a linebacker tackle. She wrapped her arms around him, tears of joy streaming down her face. The pain in her ankle was nothing compared to the pain she'd feel in a world without Ollie.

Isaiah dropped down beside them. His own eyes were suspiciously bright. "Are you two all right?"

Addie lifted her arm to touch the blood streaming down his scarred cheek from a wound on his temple. "You're bleeding."

He glanced at her arm. Concern flashed across his face. "So are you."

She cast her eyes at her arm. "I'd forgotten that. When he shot at me, he grazed my arm."

Now that he'd reminded her, she winced. The area was raw and throbbing. "I don't think it's deep."

"It'll leave a scar."

She heard the sorrow in his tone. "A scar means I survived. I'll never regret its presence."

He met her eyes one more time before sweeping them both in his arms. She rested her forehead against his arm, trying to stem the flow of tears.

"Mommy, why are you crying?"

She choked, trying to respond past the emotion clogging her throat and filling her sinuses. Every time she opened her mouth to speak, to reassure him that she was fine, a broken sob fell from her lips.

"Your mother's happy, Ollie," Isaiah said, his own words raw like a rusty chainsaw. "She was worried about you, but now that she knows you're fine, she's feeling emotional."

She wasn't the only one, she wanted to say.

A flurry of footsteps stomping through the snow shattered the mood. Paramedics swarmed around them. They lifted Addie's leg and removed the boot from her injured leg. Agony shot through her. She cried out, shocked.

"Mommy!"

"Your mother is fine, Ollie. Come with me." Isaiah's smooth voice dribbled over her senses, calming her. Ollie subsided, sniffing. She watched him lead her son to another paramedic. Good. He'd be checked out, too. She knew he had to be freezing. And he needed his insulin. She sat up too quickly and smothered another cry.

"Isaiah! He needs his insulin."

The smile drained from the paramedic's face. Low insulin was not something to take lightly.

Isaiah waved his arms as if brushing away the worry filling the atmosphere. "I took care of it. When I noticed you were gone and realized something was wrong, I grabbed an apple and gave it to him when he found me."

The paramedic sighed. "Good to hear. You might have saved his life."

"He did," Addie said, suddenly tired now that the adrenalin that had fueled her system for the past few hours drained away. She fought against the urge to lie back and let herself fall into a deep sleep.

"Don't forget her arm," she heard Isaiah's voice murmur. "A bullet grazed it."

Now that he'd reminded her, she became aware of a throbbing ache in her bicep. It wasn't nearly as bad as her ankle.

"She'll be fine, Isaiah." Micah had arrived. Now Isaiah wouldn't be alone to face the fallout.

It was no good. She was too tired to stay awake. Ollie was with Isaiah. They were both alive and well, and Micah would see that they didn't have any repercussions with the law. Now that her brother-in-law was out of the way, the contract out on her was void. She had time. With a sigh, she surrendered to the darkness beckoning her.

She came awake in fits and starts. Gradually, her eyes fluttered open and remained that way. Glancing to her right, she realized she was hooked up to a monitor. An IV was connected to the back of her hand. Probably morphine for the pain. She glanced down. Her feet were under the hospital blanket, but she could tell the one was bulkier than the other.

"It's not broken."

Her head whipped to the right. Her heartbeat galloped in her chest. They might not like that at the nurses' station.

Isaiah. She drank in his features. They hadn't changed, but she saw a new softness in his eyes. She couldn't help but respond to that look. Then she recalled his words.

"My ankle isn't broken?"

"A bad sprain, but it will be fine. It's wrapped. And your arm will heal. They're mostly worried because you lost so much blood. You should be able to leave tomorrow morning. Which is good, right?" He dropped his gaze, no longer looking at her.

She nodded, a frown turning her lips down. What wasn't he telling her? "Where's Ollie?"

He rubbed the back of his neck. "Well, your husband's mother arrived."

"What?" She had to have heard him wrong. "His mother? I didn't know she was still alive. I have never met her."

"She said as much. She said she and your

husband had been estranged most of his life. She didn't give the details. But she's staying at the Plain and Simple Bed and Breakfast in town. She wanted Ollie to stay with her, being a blood relative and all, but Micah and I put that idea off the table. He's with my parents. They're spoiling him, but taking good care to monitor his diabetes. We have allowed her to visit with him, but always supervised. Ollie will go nowhere with no one unless you approve it."

That relieved some of her concern, but not all. Why wouldn't he look at her?

"Isaiah, what's going through your mind?"

"You."

A flush covered her face. Still, something wasn't right.

Finally, their gazes collided, his expression tortured. Then she understood. He'd killed someone. He'd broken his oath for her.

"You're going away," said Addison.

He winced. Then nodded. "Not permanently. I have feelings for you, Addison Bruce Johnson. Strong ones. But my head isn't in a good place. I need some time."

Her heart ached in her chest. She heard what he was saying, but wanted to scream. How did she know he'd ever find that peace he sought? And how long was some time? A few days?

Weeks? Months? How long would she wait for him?

He was worth it, though.

"I have strong feelings for you, too, Isaiah. Please come back to me. We have so much to talk about."

He smiled. It was the saddest smile she'd ever seen, and it nearly broke her heart. "I will. When I can."

She couldn't speak. She'd woken up to the joy of his presence, and then he destroyed her within a few minutes.

He slowly pushed himself to a standing position, the chair creaking slightly. When he moved closer, she held her breath. He leaned over and touched his lips to hers, gently brushing them back and forth. It was so soft, it was barely a kiss. When he started to lift his head away, she brought her unfettered hand to his cheek. He covered it with his own. Then lowered his head and kissed her again, deeper.

She tasted salt. Their tears mingled. He swiped his hand across his face. Then his thumbs gently smoothed her tears from her cheeks. He pressed a final kiss to her forehead like a benediction.

Then he was gone, leaving a gaping hole in her life only he could fill.

SEVENTEEN

Three days after Christmas, he'd had enough. He had left Addie and Oliver fourteen days ago and had been miserable every day since. His family had noticed. Gideon had glared at him over breakfast Saturday morning.

"What?" Isaiah demanded after they had left the house and headed to the barn.

Gideon waved a dismissive hand. "I'm getting tired of being the only smart man in the family."

Isaiah halted in his tracks. "Whoa. Gid, what brought that on?"

For the life of him, he couldn't think of how he'd offended his ever-cheerful and most mischievous brother.

"I'll tell you what." Gideon crossed his arms across his chest. "You, Micah and Zeke all fell in love with these beautiful women who love you back, *ja*? Then you walk away from them. I have to be the one to tell you to embrace this gift from *Gott*. Why?"

"At least you can thank your older brother for showing you what not to do when you fall in love."

He'd meant to lighten the atmosphere. The surge of pain that crossed Gideon's face nearly made him step back.

"I won't ever get married. Not now."

Isaiah was stunned. Not so much by Gideon's words as by the anger emanating from his sibling. This was about more than his relationship with Addie. This was about Gideon, pure and simple. Gideon and the broken heart he never showed anyone.

"Who was she, Gideon?" he asked, compassion filling him for the other man's suffering.

Gideon shook his head. "It doesn't matter. She's no longer an option for me. I thought she would be my *frau* one day. She made a choice that made that impossible."

Isaiah bit back his questions, knowing he couldn't pry into Gideon's pain. Maybe when they knew each other better, Gid would open up more. Isaiah had heard enough to make a guess. Either she left the Amish church, or she chose someone else. Either way, Gideon was right. His love was truly out of his reach.

Isaiah could have kicked himself. Gideon was correct. He was making the same mistake Micah had made. Throwing his arm around his brother's shoulder, he gently squeezed then let him go. "You are absolutely right. I'm an idiot. Can you tell our parents that I had to take care of something?"

"Gladly." Gideon gave him a sad smile. "Don't mess this up, okay? I think Addie would make a wonderful *gut* sister."

He agreed. She'd make an even better wife, if he could convince her to accept him. Now that he'd come to a decision, he made a mad dash to his car, his churning boots spitting and splashing mud and snow over his pants. He didn't care. Addie was all that mattered.

Forty minutes later, he pulled up in front of her house and put the car in Park. All the hope that had built up inside him drained, leaving devastation in its wake.

She was gone.

Isaiah stared at the SOLD sign in front of Addie's house. He didn't need to knock on the door to know it was already empty. Her car wasn't in the driveway. The heavy drapes had been taken down, and the Christmas tree that had stood in the middle of the window the first time he'd been there was gone, as if it had never been there.

It was like she'd been erased again.

Isaiah rubbed his chest, attempting to dislodge the emptiness growing inside. He had messed up again, and this time he wasn't sure he could fix it. Sure, he had told Addie that he needed his space to heal and get a chance to be part of the Bender family again. He had been broken for most of his life. That couldn't be fixed in the space of the week they'd been together.

What he hadn't expected was that she wouldn't wait for him. That he would come back and find she'd sold the house and left without him. Hadn't he expressed that he intended to return?

He recalled Micah sitting him down and telling him how he had met and nearly lost Lissa and Shelby. Had nearly lost the chance to have them in his life when he had left her waiting and wondering. But this was different. Isaiah had only been gone for a couple of weeks.

Christmas had come and gone, but he had hoped they could be together to begin the new year.

His dreams crumbled to dust around him.

Wait. He might have lost her forever. But he'd been a bounty hunter long enough to have the skills to track her down again. Maybe if he found her, he could prove to her that his love was real. That he wouldn't abandon her.

He also had to let her know that he was willing to give up his life of danger and excitement. It had grown old, chasing fugitives, not coming home every night.

He'd have to find a new job. But he could do that. He was skilled with guns, tracking and using technology. He also had good hands-on experience. And he was willing to learn. If he needed to find a different career to have Addie and Ollie back, he'd do it.

In his heart, they were his family. He'd do anything to have them back.

Letting his chin sink to his chest, he did the only thing he could do. He lifted up his heart in prayer, knowing that if he and Addie were meant to be together, he'd require God's help. Suddenly, he recalled the verse his father used to quote when he and his brothers were young and needed help with a difficulty that was out of their parents' hands.

"Ask, and it shall be given you; seek, and ye shall find; knock, and it shall be opened unto you."

He was pretty sure it was from the gospels. Grabbing his phone, he looked it up.

"Ah. Matthew 7:7."

He read the verse to himself.

Ask, and it shall be given you; seek, and ye shall find; knock, and it shall be opened unto you.

He leaned his head back against the headrest and let his eyelids drop. "Lord, You know my heart. I love Addison and want to make her my wife one day. I want to be a father for little Oliver. I believe You have a plan for us, but she's gone. I could find her, but I am afraid I might lose her if I take too long. I ask, I beg for Your help. If it is good for us to be together, please show me what to do."

He sat in that position for a while, opening his heart and pouring out his soul. When he had no more words to say, he let out a breath and rested in the peace brought from the purging. He hadn't expected God to show up and heal him in such a noticeable way, but his chest felt lighter than it had in years.

Someone knocked on his window. He startled and choked back a surprised yell. He'd been so wrapped up in his own head, he'd failed to notice the older woman approaching. She looked about his mother's age. Her gray-flecked black hair was covered by a faux-fur-trimmed dark blue scarf. Matching gloves covered her hands. Her face was what caught and held his attention. She had the kindest smile he'd ever seen.

Hitting the button on his door, the power window lowered, letting in the freezing air. His breath puffed in front of his face. "May I help you?"

Her smile widened. "Actually, I think I can help you, dear." She pulled an envelope from her pocket. "Are you Isaiah?"

The hope that had died when he saw the SOLD sign sprang to life once more. There was only one person who would have told her his name.

"I am. Did Addie tell you about me?"

"She told me enough. She said you'd be coming by the house one day. If I happened to see you, I was to give you this." She held the envelope out to him.

He paled. "What if you hadn't seen me?"

"I asked her that. She said she knew where your family lived. If she didn't hear from you by New Year's Day, she'd mail a letter there."

Addie had planned on reaching out to him. He reached out and took the letter from her fingers. He was so filled with wonder there was no room for embarrassment that she saw his hands shaking with the strength of his emotions.

With a final smile, she tugged her scarf closer around her face and returned to her own house across the street. Isaiah waited just long enough to be sure she'd made it safely inside her home without slipping on the icy slush before tearing open the envelope.

Dear Isaiah,
I know it will shock you seeing the house sold when you come back. Please know, I have every faith that you will, because you said you would.

I'm sorry I can't be here. I got notified that I needed to be in Seattle to deal with the fallout from my late brother-in-law's poor choices. I'll explain it to you when I see you.

I should return after the first of January. I'm not sure of the exact date yet. I'll call you then if I don't hear from you before then.
Until then.
Addie

Seattle. He didn't have anything more than that. No address. No zip code. He did, however, know her brother-in-law's name. It might be enough to locate her. How many Addison Bruces could there be in the country who were staying in Seattle?

It didn't matter. If she was there, he'd find her.

He'd never failed to find someone he was searching for. But this time, he had God on his side.

"Mommy, when can we go home?" Oliver asked, crunching into his taco. She handed him a napkin to wipe the juice from his chin. She glanced around the hotel restaurant, checking to see if anyone was near enough to listen in on their conversation.

Stop. You're free. No one is chasing you. It's time to stop looking over your shoulder.

It sounded good. In reality, though, it would be a long time before she felt comfortable sitting out in the open. If Ollie hadn't been so sick of the hotel suite, she would have ordered room service again. But she had been ready to climb the walls as well. It wasn't healthy, living in a cage. Even an expensive one.

"I don't know when we can leave here. But remember what we talked about yesterday? We have to find a new home. The one we lived in is someone else's home now."

She hadn't expected the place to sell so fast. She had no regrets. After being attacked in that house, and knowing that Tricia had died in the house next door, she never wanted to set foot in it again. It held too many traumatic memories.

He nodded, his mouth full. She waited until he chewed and swallowed. Knowing Oliver, there were more questions to come.

"If we can't live there, could we live with Mr. Isaiah?"

Addie choked on her iced tea. How to answer that innocent query? In her heart, she wanted to say nothing would please her more than to marry the complicated man she'd fallen head over heels in love with. But she couldn't. While she believed he had feelings for her, she couldn't be sure it was enough. And she would never pressure him to make a choice before he was ready.

"I don't think so, honey. I think we'll have to find a new home close to a good school where you can go to kindergarten next year." She pasted what she hoped was an enthusiastic smile on her face. "Won't that be exciting?

You'll be able to choose how you want to decorate your room!"

He shrugged, unconvinced.

Sighing, she slumped back in her chair. "I can't promise you we'll be able to leave tomorrow, but how about a compromise? You don't complain today, and we can go swimming this afternoon."

She was somewhat shocked when he didn't immediately brighten up. He'd been asking to swim all morning. Now that the offer was on the table, he squinted his eyes and considered the idea. "I guess we could do that."

Suddenly, she laughed. No matter what happened, Ollie always cheered her up. He was a blessing, for sure.

Ollie's head jerked up, and a wide, brilliant smile bloomed on his round face. "Mr. Isaiah!"

Addie spun in her seat. Her heart pounded in her chest. Isaiah, the man who had stolen her heart, sauntered toward them. His nonchalant posture didn't fool her. She read the uncertainty in the lines carved around his mouth. He had tracked her down, but wasn't sure of his reception. Had he gotten her letter?

She'd been emotionally exhausted when she'd written it. She couldn't recall exactly what she had said but was pretty sure she had told him she would see him when she arrived home.

Why hadn't he texted her?

He strode to their table, halting in front of it.

"Mr. Isaiah!" Oliver launched himself at his hero, catching the man off guard. Isaiah swooped him into his arms for a quick hug and then deposited him back on the restaurant floor. Giggling, Ollie dropped back into his seat, his eyes shining.

"Are you staying with us? Mommy says new people are living in our house. Can we come live with you?"

Heat burst onto her cheeks. "Ollie! You don't ask people things like that."

Slanting her gaze up at Isaiah, she observed his complexion appeared flushed, as well.

"I saw that your house was sold. And I met a very kind lady who lived across the street from your old house."

Good. He'd received her letter.

"I do want to talk with your mom for a few moments, if that's all right with you?" he asked Ollie, but his gaze remained fastened on her.

"Yeah. That's fine." Ollie graciously gave his approval.

"Let's go up to the suite," she suggested. "I can put on a movie for Ollie, and we can talk."

"What about swimming?" Ollie reminded her.

"I haven't forgotten. But you can't swim right after you eat anyway."

They made their way to the elevator, Ollie running ahead, leading the way.

"Is that true, that you're not supposed to swim after you've eaten?" Isaiah wondered idly, his hand brushing hers as they walked. "Because we always swam after we ate a picnic lunch when I was a kid. In the creek behind our house."

She tried to ignore the fluttering inside her belly. He was here. They were practically holding hands. The temptation to grab his hand was great. She resisted, however. They needed to talk. If they had no future, she didn't want to risk her heart, or her son's, any more than she already had.

"I don't know if it's true or an old wives' tale. It suited my purposes, so I won't complain."

When they reached the suite, she grimaced. "It's far too fancy, but this is where the lawyers put us while we are here."

"Lawyers?"

"I'll explain in a moment."

They entered the majestic suite. It was nearly a small apartment. There were two bedrooms, a kitchenette, a bathroom with a Jacuzzi and a small sitting area with a seventy-two-inch television and a small balcony. She didn't even want to know how much such a place cost per night. As soon as all the red tape cleared, she and Ollie would be on their way back to Sutter Springs to find a more permanent home.

She didn't want to think about what part Isaiah would play in their decisions.

Within five minutes, Ollie had picked out the movie he wanted, and she was streaming it through the smart TV. She gestured for Isaiah to follow her and led him to the couch in the main room. "He can't leave without walking past us here."

Isaiah didn't immediately sit. He paced the room for a few minutes, clearly uncomfortable. She watched him for a while without speaking. She knew what was in her heart, what she wanted. Who she wanted. She reminded herself of the first line of her favorite scripture verse, 1 Corinthians 13:4. *"Charity suffereth long, and is kind."* Isaiah hadn't lived in a world where these virtues were treasured for very long. As much as she wanted to begin speaking, to express what was in her heart to him, she would be patient and kind. She would wait until he was ready to receive all she had to give. He was totally worth waiting for.

His shoulders squared. He spun to face her, locking her in place with the intensity of his gaze. Her pulse sped up in reaction.

"I was wrong."

She blinked. "Wrong? Wrong about what?" *Please don't say you were wrong about us.* She wouldn't be able to take it if he broke her heart now that her hopes were set on them having a future.

"I told you I needed to go and get my head on straight. I needed healing, that much is true. But then I left you, and even though I had my family, I wasn't complete. My heart nearly stopped when I drove to your house three days ago and found you were gone."

She bit her lip. Hurting him had never been in her agenda. "I didn't want to go, but I needed to close down this part of my life before I could move on."

He came to sit next to her. "Do you love me?"

She stiffened, suddenly feeling vulnerable. She thought he loved her. Why would he ask if he didn't? But being the first to say it felt risky.

He was worth it. She drew in a deep breath, strengthening her resolve to be bold.

"Wait." He held up his hand. "That's not a fair question. First, let me tell you that I am in love with you, Addison Bruce Johnson. I adore your son. I want nothing more than to marry you and have a family with you."

"I love you, too, Isaiah." She reached for his hands and held them tight. "All I want is to be your wife."

He gently pulled one hand free and used it to brush a hair from her face. "You know I'm still dealing with my past."

"I know." She shrugged. "I'm still in the middle of this mess here."

He searched her face. "I'm here. I won't leave unless you tell me to. Is this something I can help you with?"

She looked so tired. Bloodshot eyes gazed back at him. And her face. It was so pale. His heart ached to hold her, to comfort her and help all her hurts go away.

But this was something she had to deal with. He'd support her in any way he could and be her strength, if she'd allow it.

She sighed, her glance skittering to the area where Oliver remained entranced by his movie. "I found out why Robert Johnson put a contract out on me. And why he tried to set me up."

He straightened in his seat. "Tell me."

"It's all so sordid." She grimaced. "Here goes. I never knew any of this until this week. When my husband was four years old, his parents split up. It was an ugly, bitter divorce. And apparently both parents wanted full custody. Finally, they decided to each take one child. My husband went with his mother, and Robert went with his father."

Isaiah couldn't believe what he was hearing. "The parents both gave up one of their children?"

She nodded. "It sounds unreal. I know. Apparently, Bill's father had a bit of a mean streak. Anyways, Bill's mom had some mental health issues. His dad was angry that their lawyers were counseling them to accept the split. He wanted both kids and saw such an agreement as a loss. Then when the judge ordered it, he had Bill's mother sign something stating she would make no efforts to see Robert, or interfere in his life in any way, or else he'd make sure she lost both kids, permanently. I guess she was scared enough to keep her distance from her other son. Which meant my husband and his brother never saw each other again. Not until four and a half years ago."

His eyes narrowed. "Right before your husband was killed."

"You got it. You see, their grandfather had built a luxury hotel chain. This," she waved a hand to indicate their lush surroundings, "is one of the hotels. When Bill's parents divorced, his grandparents didn't approve of the way things were handled. Robert had believed he'd inherit the entire chain. He had grown up believing it would all be his one day. He didn't want the hotels. He wanted to sell them to pay off his debts. So, when his dad died, he went into the lawyers' meeting expecting to receive an inheritance, only to be told by his grandmother and the lawyers that the hotel business was to be split between him and his long lost brother."

Isaiah whistled. "Did he know where his brother was?"

She shook her head. "No, but his grandparents had kept in touch with Bill's mom. They didn't agree with the custody arrangement and hated that they were denied knowing both their grandsons. I think they thought it would be the way to mend the gap. If Robert didn't get Bill to agree, a cousin would inherit it all."

"He couldn't pay off the debts if your husband didn't agree to sell."

"Correct. My husband was all for selling and splitting the profits. I can only imagine he thought the money would come in handy after the baby was born. But Robert didn't want that. He didn't think Bill should get any money since he was raised with his mother. He wanted Bill to sign away his half so Robert could sell and collect everything. When my husband didn't go for it, he killed him, or had him killed, figuring then he'd have it all."

"But you inherited your husband's share."

"Yep." She stood and moved to the refrigerator unit. She took out a couple of bottled waters and sauntered back. After handing one to him, she opened hers and took a long drink. "I knew nothing of it. Somehow the letter from the lawyer got misplaced. I have no proof Robert did anything."

"Why did he stalk you?"

"He stalked me to see if he could find out anything to use against me to pressure me to sell. There wasn't anything, unless he kidnapped my son. But then there was the chance it would backfire. So, he decided to set me up. If I was in jail, he thought I would lose my inheritance. But then he found out the only way I would lose it was if I were dead. He convinced his friend to contract a bounty hunter."

"So if the hired killers failed to find you, he would still be able to kill you once I brought you in."

"He didn't plan on hiring you at first. It was only after he found out that I wouldn't lose my inheritance. I had to be completely out of the picture for him to inherit. When you didn't find me immediately, he put a price on my head to ensure someone did the job. And then Chad realized I was innocent and started making waves, so he killed him, as well."

He shook his head. "How did you find out all of this?"

She snorted. "Robert had confessed his whole plan to his girlfriend. When she was arrested as an accomplice, she spilled the beans. Told the police everything."

"Wow."

"And now I own all the hotels."

His head swung around, and he stared at her, his mouth open. "What?"

"Isn't that absurd? So, this week, I came here to sell them. I have a buyer. I don't need the money. In my mind, it's blood money. My husband was killed for it, and we were nearly victims, too. I signed papers yesterday to do-

nate the money to diabetes research. All of it."
The last part was said with a touch of defiance.

He sagged against the back of the couch. "I
wasn't going to tell you what to do. But I am
so glad to hear this. I know most people would
tell you to keep some of the money, but I'm
with you. It's tainted."

She dropped her gaze for a moment, taking his hand in her own and gently running
her fingers over the back of it. "There is one
thing that I regret more than anything else in
all this."

He straightened. After coming all this way,
he didn't want to hear that she couldn't have
him in her life. He controlled the shaking rack-
ing his soul. "What do you regret?"

Her gentle gaze captured his. He saw no re-
jection. Only pure, shining love. The fear fell to
the wayside. "You had to kill Robert. Because
of me, you broke your promise to yourself."

His heart, so used to being alone, skipped
a beat in his chest. Warmth filled him at the
evidence of her care. "I didn't break my promise. If he hadn't been an immediate threat to
you and Oliver, Robert would still be alive.
He'd be rotting in a jail cell, but he'd be alive.
My promise was I would only kill to protect

someone else. To save a life. That's exactly what I did."

"You had to leave after that."

He pushed a gentle hand through her hair. "I did. I had to come to terms with the fact I had taken a life. And the fact that my family wanted me back. Christina—Joss—was back. And I had to come to terms with you."

She shifted away from him, wariness on her face. "With me?"

"Sweetheart, you and Ollie are the most important people in my world. But I live in a world of danger. I couldn't be a bounty hunter and continue to court you. But law and justice are what I am called to. I am convinced God gave me a calling."

"Where does that leave us?"

"Well, I talked to Henry. His security business is taking off, and he offered me a job as a partner. It wouldn't be as exciting, but I would be protecting people, and I would come home every night."

When a smile lifted her lips, his breath froze. She came to stand beside him. He stood. "I don't have a ring yet. I was in such a rush to get to you that I didn't stop and get one." He went down on one knee. "Even without a

ring, will you have me? Will you be my wife
and let me adopt Ollie as our son?"

She nodded, tears welling up in her eyes.
When he stood, she threw her arms around his
neck. Hugging her tight, he squeezed his lids
tight to keep his own emotions at bay. When
he was back in control, he loosened his grip.
Only enough to lean down and kiss her the
way he dreamed about. When he felt her generous response, his whole being flooded with
love and gratitude for the precious woman in
his embrace.

EPILOGUE

"Okay, second graders, it's time to clean up. Table leaders, please take the paint trays to the side counters."

Addie supervised the students as they took their art projects to the drying racks designated for their class. A couple of girls needed to be encouraged to move faster. When the class was once again in order, she smiled. A quick peek at the clock on the wall told her it was time to release them.

"Nice job, friends! We will finish this project when I see you next week. Please line up at the door and remember your hallway expectations."

Eighteen second graders lined up with some giggling. She smiled. She couldn't blame them. They had one more week before Christmas break began. She was excited for the holidays, too. What a difference a year made.

Opening the door, she greeted Sami, the second-grade teacher. Sami had also become a dear friend. She was energetic and funny with an open heart that had welcomed her into the school without reservation. "They're all yours!"

"Thanks, Addie!" Sami waved her class into the hall. "Go to the end of the hall and stop at the corner."

The students filed out. As they passed, some of them waved at Addie. "Bye, Mrs. Bender."

She waved back. "Bye! I'll see you next week!"

Addie and Sami observed their progress, making sure the students stayed near the wall and kept their hands to themselves. When the line halted at the corner, Sami turned back to Addie with a grin. "If I don't see you before you leave, have fun with the in-laws this weekend!"

"Will do."

A gusty sigh, half happy, half tired, escaped. Then she laughed to herself and returned to her room. Second grade was her last class of the day. She straightened up her room, cleaning the brushes and wiping down tables until the announcements began. They were preceded by a loud squeal. She winced.

The door flew open. Oliver charged inside, his backpack banging against the heels of his new boots. "Oliver Bender, didn't I tell you not to drag your bag on the ground?"

He slid to a halt, his shoes making skid marks on the floor. "Sorry."

When he flashed his grin at her, she melted, but made an attempt to hide it. He was getting too sure of himself. "Pick it up and put it on your back the right way. We need to get out of here as soon as we can today."

He bounced on his toes. "We are going to see Grandma and Grandpa Bender today, right?"

"Right." She tousled his hair. He was growing up too fast. Her little guy was almost halfway through his kindergarten year. And in two months, he'd turn six years old. She could barely believe it. She was blessed they had an opening for an art teacher in the school district she and Isaiah had moved into last May, right after they got married.

She grinned, thinking about their wedding. It had been perfect. Isaiah wanted his brother Micah to be his best man. Micah became too emotional to do more than nod when Isaiah asked him. Unfortunately, he couldn't have Zeke or Gideon stand up with him as it wasn't an Amish wedding. Instead, Steve, Henry and Zack had done the honors. She had enjoyed meeting his former military friends.

Joss and Lissa had both been bridesmaids. Addie loved all her sisters-in-law. The last two bridesmaids had come as a surprise. She'd been thrilled when Lorraine and Mary Beth Karns had agreed to stand up with her. Addie had been pleased to become acquainted with Jerry's brother, Scott, after she returned to Sutter Springs. When he had introduced his wife, Mary Beth, the two women had bonded instantly. She and Lorraine had already started to develop a lasting friendship. In fact, sometimes the three women would sit together when she and Isaiah got together with Scott, Jerry and their wives. She, Mary Beth and Lorraine would whisper and giggle. So much so that the men watched them with narrow eyes, obviously wondering if they were being discussed.

Once they were wed, Isaiah had adopted Oliver so they all had the same last name. Oliver knew about Bill, and they were very open in answering all of his questions. But the adoption gave him a solid place in the family. And besides, Isaiah adored him as if he were his own son. They just made it legal.

"Daddy will be home by the time we get there, so let's get a move on."

"Yay! Bonus Daddy time!"

Laughing at his antics, she followed her son, locking the classroom door behind her. The halls were clearing out. Most of the teachers were leaving immediately after the buses departed due to the heavy snow in the forecast. She and Isaiah had planned on going to see his parents tomorrow for the monthly family get together. However, the snow had changed their plans. Since Sunday was supposed to be nice out, they decided to make it a weekend trip and come home Sunday afternoon.

"Will Shelby be there?"

She grinned. "Yes. I talked with your Aunt Lissa this morning. She and Uncle Micah are coming in tonight also. They'll bring Shelby and the baby."

Joss and Steve would also be there with their children, five-year-old Christina and two-year-old Timmy, as well as Zeke and his wife, Molly, and their young twins, Zedekiah and Deborah. Molly hadn't said anything yet, but Addie suspected she was expecting again. And, of course, Isaiah's youngest brother, Gideon, would be there, playing practical jokes and keeping them all in stitches. Ollie loved them all. But it was nine-year-old Shelby who held his young heart. Shelby was a good sport and didn't seem to mind him following her everywhere.

"I'm going to marry Shelby when I grow up," he announced.

She smacked her lips closed to keep her chuckles from leaking out. Oliver had been proclaiming he'd marry his cousin since she had married Isaiah. Shelby had been the flower girl, and Ollie had been the ring bearer. He'd asked immediately after the wedding if he and Shelby were married, too.

By the time they arrived home, there was a fine dusting of Christmas snow on the grass and the driveway. Secretly, she was thrilled. Addie couldn't imagine Christmas without snow, but the season had been unusually warm. She was looking forward to days when they had enough accumulation to make snowmen and go sledding with Ollie, followed by enjoying mugs of hot chocolate with marshmallows and then snuggling on the sofa in front of the fireplace with Isaiah while sharing their dreams of the future.

She gently touched her stomach. She hadn't told Isaiah yet, but she might have to hold off on the sledding this year. Checking the rearview mirror, she grinned at Ollie. He'd be a great older brother.

Isaiah met them at the door. Ollie got his hug first. "Your snack is on the table. Do you need help with your insulin?"

"I can do it myself, Daddy."

They watched their confident son saunter into the kitchen, rolling their eyes when his backpack hit the floor with a crash. Isaiah slid his arm around his wife's back, and they moved together to watch Ollie do his insulin. They let him do it himself, but he was supervised the entire time. He looked up to make sure they were there and then proceeded to give himself an injection with the tiny needle.

They had talked about getting him fitted with an insulin pump but had decided to wait until he was older as he would need to be able to program the device and change the cannula independently. In the past year, they'd gotten his levels under control. He rarely needed to drink juice to avoid low glucose levels.

When his snack was completed and he'd cleaned up after himself, Addie kissed the curls on the top of his head. "Okay, buddy. Head upstairs to your room and get your things. I want to leave here in fifteen minutes. Got it?"

"Got it!" He zoomed out of the room. "We're going to see Shelby!"

Isaiah chuckled and gathered his wife into his arms. "Finally, a moment of privacy."

"Oh?" She leaned back to see his face and arched her eyebrows. "What do we need privacy for, Mr. Bender?"

He gave her a mock growl. "For this, Mrs. Bender."

Tugging her closer, he leaned down and kissed her. What started as a sweet kiss deepened, the richness of their love infusing it with warmth and passion.

"Eww. Why do you always smooch when I leave the room?"

They broke apart laughing.

"Let's go." Isaiah motioned for his son to go ahead of them. "You can ask embarrassing questions in the car."

Within moments, the small family had locked the house and begun the journey to Isaiah's childhood home.

"Does it feel strange?" she asked him, once Oliver was occupied with his sketch pad.

"What?"

"Returning to where you grew up after all these years?" They'd talked about his past several times. Addie understood why he'd made the choices he had, but she'd always wondered if some of the hurt carried over into his current relationship with his family.

"Not weird, precisely." He merged onto the highway. "I regret that I missed seeing my brothers grow up. Especially Zeke. He and I have talked, and it was hardest on him because the two of us had been close at one point. I also regret not being there when Joss returned. But I've accepted it. I can't change it. My parents never gave up on me. Micah told me that during the years I was away, they never gave up. If someone mentioned me and said I was 'a lost soul,' my mother would calmly say God would bring me back. And He did."

He did, indeed. Although, they had probably expected him to return to his Amish heritage. But too much had happened in his life for that. So they opened their arms to him as he was.

"I'm glad you have them in your life again."

He reached over and took her hand. Lifting it to his lips, he kissed her knuckles. "I'm happy that I have you in my life, too."

Warmth filled her heart. She never doubted his complete devotion to her. Not once. That was who he was. Once he committed himself, he was all in.

She was tempted to tell him her secret while

they were in the car, but held back. She wanted to tell him when it was just the two of them, and then they could tell Ollie together.

It was twilight when Isaiah pulled into his old home. Tilting her head, she smiled at him. His eyes shone, lit by an inner joy. The moment Addie opened his car door, Oliver bounded from his seat and dashed up the stairs to the porch and into his grandmother's embrace.

"*Ack!* Who is this big boy? It can't be my little Oliver, say? If I squeeze real hard, maybe I can make him small again."

Ollie giggled when Edith Bender squeezed him. Nathan Bender stepped beside his wife and greeted Isaiah and Addie. "*Welkum.* Were the roads bad?"

"They were fine, *Daed.*" Isaiah bypassed his father's outstretched hand and swooped in for a hug. He had confessed to Addie when they got married that since he'd missed years of affection from his family, he was going to do his best to recoup his losses.

Nathan's eyes glazed with tears. He thumped his third born son on the back in a man-hug. Addie shook her head, happy to see her husband and his family together. Lissa popped out behind them and made her way down the stairs to greet Addie, her one-year-old son in the crook of her elbow.

"Can I hold him?" Addie asked, holding her own arms open.

"Absolutely. Come on, MJ. Go see Aunt Addie."

The child squealed and fell into her embrace willingly. "Ann. Ann."

She raised her eyebrows at her sister-in-law. "Aunt? He's got a new word."

"More than one. I can hardly keep up with them. Of course, sometimes I'll think he's babbling, and Micah will catch what I miss."

She nodded. Lissa was profoundly deaf and wore two cochlear implants. Although she was skilled at lipreading and heard most speech sounds with the devices, Addie knew Lissa would miss some of the sounds if her back was turned or if the environment was too noisy, which made it natural for her to miss some of the new words.

The entire group swarmed through the door and spilled into the family room, where warm kerosene lamps created a pleasant glow. Edith, Addie and Lissa left the children and the men there and finished making dinner. It was a simple yet hearty feast of beef stew, homemade bread and jam, with peach cobbler for dessert. Before the meal was served, Nathan set up a small card table so there would be seats for everyone.

"I have three more tables," he announced. "We should be *gut* for the whole family tomorrow, ain't so?"

"I would imagine so, *Daed.*" Despite the fact that he had opted not to join the Amish church, Isaiah had continued to call his parents by their Amish titles rather than Mom and Dad. Addie noticed they both sparkled with joy when he did it. She had married a complicated and sensitive man.

That night, alone in their room, she told him about the baby.

"I'm going to be a father again," he whispered, delight saturating each word.

His words brought a lump to her throat. It was one more proof that in his heart, Oliver was his son, completely.

He brought her close, and she snuggled into his chest, content. God had brought them through the storm and into the sunlight. She couldn't ask for more.

He lifted her face, and their lips met in a sweet kiss that promised a lifetime of love.

* * * * *

Dear Reader,

I hope you enjoyed *Hunted at Christmas*. I love writing books about siblings. Isaiah Bender is the third Bender brother. He's a gentle warrior who has suffered much trauma in his life; I wanted to bring him home. Addie is strong with her own past anguish. Their story was a joy to write!

I love connecting with readers! You can contact me at www.danarlynn.com.

Blessings,
Dana R. Lynn

Get 3 FREE REWARDS!

We'll send you 2 FREE Books <u>plus</u> a FREE Mystery Gift.

Both the **Love Inspired®** and **Love Inspired® Suspense** series feature compelling novels filled with inspirational romance, faith, forgiveness and hope.

YES! Please send me 2 FREE novels from the Love Inspired or Love Inspired Suspense series and my FREE gift (gift is worth about $10 retail). After receiving them, if I don't wish to receive any more books, I can return the shipping statement marked "cancel." If I don't cancel, I will receive 6 brand-new Love Inspired Larger-Print books or Love Inspired Suspense Larger-Print books every month and be billed just $6.49 each in the U.S. or $6.74 each in Canada. That is a savings of at least 16% off the cover price. It's quite a bargain! Shipping and handling is just 50¢ per book in the U.S. and $1.25 per book in Canada.* I understand that accepting the 2 free books and gift places me under no obligation to buy anything. I can always return a shipment and cancel at any time by calling the number below. The free books and gift are mine to keep no matter what I decide.

Choose one: ☐ **Love Inspired**   ☐ **Love Inspired**   ☐ **Or Try Both!**
            Larger-Print   **Suspense**   (122/322 & 107/307
            (122/322 BPA GRPA)   **Larger-Print**   BPA GRRP)
                                    (107/307 BPA GRPA)

Name (please print)

Address   Apt. #

City   State/Province   Zip/Postal Code

Email: Please check this box ☐ if you would like to receive newsletters and promotional emails from Harlequin Enterprises ULC and its affiliates. You can unsubscribe anytime.

Mail to the **Harlequin Reader Service:**
IN U.S.A.: P.O. Box 1341, Buffalo, NY 14240-8531
IN CANADA: P.O. Box 603, Fort Erie, Ontario L2A 5X3

Want to try 2 free books from another series? Call 1-800-873-8635 or visit www.ReaderService.com.

Get 3 FREE REWARDS!

We'll send you 2 FREE Books **plus** a FREE Mystery Gift.

Both the **Harlequin® Special Edition** and **Harlequin® Heartwarming™** series feature compelling novels filled with stories of love and strength where the bonds of friendship, family and community unite.

YES! Please send me 2 FREE novels from the Harlequin Special Edition or Harlequin Heartwarming series and my FREE Gift (gift is worth about $10 retail). After receiving them, if I don't wish to receive any more books, I can return the shipping statement marked "cancel." If I don't cancel, I will receive 6 brand-new Harlequin Special Edition books every month and be billed just $5.49 each in the U.S. or $6.24 each in Canada, a savings of at least 12% off the cover price, or 4 brand-new Harlequin Heartwarming Larger-Print books every month and be billed just $6.24 each in the U.S. or $6.74 each in Canada, a savings of at least 19% off the cover price. It's quite a bargain! Shipping and handling is just 50¢ per book in the U.S. and $1.25 per book in Canada.* I understand that accepting the 2 free books and gift places me under no obligation to buy anything. I can always return a shipment and cancel at any time by calling the number below. The free books and gift are mine to keep no matter what I decide.

Choose one: ☐ **Harlequin Special Edition**
(235/335 BPA GRMK)

☐ **Harlequin Heartwarming Larger-Print**
(161/361 BPA GRMK)

☐ **Or Try Both!**
(235/335 & 161/361 BPA GRPZ)

Name (please print)

Address   Apt. #

City   State/Province   Zip/Postal Code

Email: Please check this box ☐ if you would like to receive newsletters and promotional emails from Harlequin Enterprises ULC and its affiliates. You can unsubscribe anytime.

Mail to the **Harlequin Reader Service:**
IN U.S.A.: P.O. Box 1341, Buffalo, NY 14240-8531
IN CANADA: P.O. Box 603, Fort Erie, Ontario L2A 5X3

Want to try 2 free books from another series? Call 1-800-873-8635 or visit www.ReaderService.com.

HSEHW23

COMING NEXT MONTH FROM
Love Inspired Suspense

SNOWBOUND ESCAPE
Pacific Northwest K-9 Unit • by Dana Mentink
Crime tech Mara Gilmore is the only eyewitness to a murder, and the real killer is determined to silence Mara for good—and frame her for the crime. Now it's up to Officer Tanner Ford and his K-9 partner to protect Mara from a vicious assailant...and an unforgiving icy wilderness.

CRIME SCENE CONSPIRACY
Texas Crime Scene Cleaners • by Jessica R. Patch
A string of staged deaths forces Texas Ranger Emily O'Connell on a covert mission to investigate a governor's connection to the deceased women. No one can know what she's doing—including former ranger Stone Spencer. But when Emily becomes the next target, she must choose between her secrets...and her life.

ABDUCTED AT CHRISTMAS
by Rhonda Starnes
Hadley Logan went into hiding to safeguard her child—but suddenly her house is breached and she's attacked by an intruder. With Christmas approaching, can Hadley risk everything to accept the protection security specialist Ryan Vincent offers...as a deadly enemy closes in?

KILLER CHRISTMAS EVIDENCE
Deputies of Anderson County • by Sami A. Abrams
When Detective Kyle Howard rescues a woman from a burning house, he's shocked that it's Cassidy Bowman—the detective who was responsible for his fiancée's death. Now Cassidy can't remember who she is...or just how close she is to finding a merciless serial killer.

MARKED TO DIE
by Kathleen Tailer
After her young daughter is poisoned—along with others—investigative reporter Eleni Townsend wants answers...especially when an attempt on her life is made. Now with danger on her trail, can FBI agent Chris Springfield help Eleni evade hit men long enough to discover the truth of her past?

DEADLY YELLOWSTONE SECRETS
by Kari Trumbo
Naturalist Tamala Roth finds herself targeted by a poacher in Yellowstone National Park who will stop at nothing to keep his secret. The only person she can trust is Ranger Clint Jackson. But when a blizzard traps them, will they make it out alive?

LISCNM0923

HARLEQUIN
PLUS

Try the best multimedia
subscription service for romance
readers like you!

Read, Watch and Play.

Experience the easiest way to get
the romance content you crave.

Start your **FREE TRIAL** at
<u>www.harlequinplus.com/freetrial</u>.